Rising Storm

Eliza Renton

Rising Storm

Fear keeps them apart. Danger binds them together.

Following his divorce, Storm focused on his job at Sentinel Security, appreciating, and enjoying to the full his return to single life. But everything changes when Jenna joins the team as their new medic. She's gorgeous, dedicated and easy to talk to, and he's hooked from their first kiss.

Jenna moved to New York for a fresh start, vowing to keep her distance from players like Storm. She'd been burned before and almost lost her son. But as she gets to know the man with the toe-curling kiss, she begins to question her strictly friends' policy.

Just as they're beginning to work things out, someone starts targeting everyone they care about, and until Storm can eliminate the threat, he'll do anything to protect Jenna and her son. As the danger escalates, they must confront their personal demons and the enemy before claiming the happiness they deserve.

Eliza's note on language in this book

Dear Reader,

I agonized over what I am about to tell you. Tom, Jenna's son, is from London. But that's not what kept this author awake at night. Believe it or not, it was whether Tom should call Jenna mum, as he would, or mom, as he will probably learn to do as they build their home in the US.

In the interest of authenticity, I settled on mum. I understand, for some, this will read like a spelling mistake or set your teeth on edge, and while I wish your ears every good health, and certainly try my best not to make spelling errors, I couldn't twist Tom's tongue around something unnatural. Mmm, like Storm says, "that didn't quite come out the way I intended."

Thanks for your patience. Happy reading!

Acknowledgements

It gets a little crazy when you're writing a book, particularly when characters refuse to talk to you or won't shut up. Times like that, I'm grateful for my writing group, The Saturday Ladies Book Club for not letting me give up, and shoving my bum back on the seat. When I just want out of my head, the women of our Thursday Sit and Knit group keep me sane. Thank you.

Contents

Chapter One

Another stakeout. Slam in the middle of Al-Shabaab's territory, Somalia, waiting for the target to play their losing hand. They always did.

Meanwhile, Storm seized another mind-numbing moment. *Stakeouts—fun for all the family.* They should emblazon that shit on a ball cap. Back to doodling in his dog-eared notebook, he wet his pencil with the tip of his tongue. Every one of his squiggles morphed into the contours of Jenna's perfect body. He traced the curves of her perfect ass and added a touch of shading under the breasts of Sentinel's gorgeous medical officer.

Self-inflicted torture, but healthier than smoking or sucking on candy. If only he hadn't messed up the other night and kissed her. He should have read the signs, realized she needed more time.

In this blistering heat, he would sacrifice a finger for a moment of icy wind. Reaching for his canteen, he took a swig of water.

At least the pay at Sentinel made up for the shit he and his team endured on the company's behalf. *You love it.* His smile earned an eyebrow raise from Winter.

"Buy a fucking bed. Any bed," Trigger said.

His friend's eyelids hovered at half-mast. If he didn't know the ex-Royal Marine better, Storm would swear his teammate had nodded off. It must have been ten minutes since he posed the bed question. He pushed out a suffering sigh. "Man, it's not that simple."

"The fuck it ain't." Frustration simmered behind Trig's black eyes.

The heat always made the fucker grumpy. Shifting sideways, Storm stretched his legs in his bud's direction. "No, my friend. There are big beds. I'm leaning that way. Soft beds, water beds, and beds that contour a woman's body." He waved his hands around an imaginary torso. "And there are... Bottom line, you need to get out more."

Trig's head shuddered on his shoulders, begging him to get on with it.

"Stop right there, fuckhead. I get plenty of bed time. Anyhow, at the rate you bang, you'll kill the springs in a week. Buy a cheap futon and auto-order a new one every three months." Trigger reasoned. "Problem eliminated."

"Tut, tut." Storm shook his head. "Winter, you're the senior here. Been banging, as Trig eloquently puts it, longer than any of us. What do you reckon?"

"Wouldn't have a clue. Ever since Maggie moved into mine, sex in a bed hasn't come up much." Winter tipped the beak of his cap from his eyes. "Overrated compared to loving my woman in the shower, on the floor, couch, countertop."

Storm stroked his chin, envious of how Winter's granite profile softened whenever he spoke of Maggie. Several years younger, she adored the big feller. "Maybe I should get one of those blow-up sex dolls."

"Watch your mouth," Winter growled.

"Okay, okay. Easy. Joke."

"Yeah, well. I'm shit sure you need to focus on something other than where you stick your dick next." Winter pointed two fingers at his eyes and raised his chin at the houses up ahead. "The sooner we take care of this fucker, Hassan, the quicker we can all get bed cozy. Or in my case, Maggie has taken a shine to our new hammock."

Storm leaned in. Keen to tell the old feller, snorting was not a great look. Hell, he would dribble next.

"Who do you think you're kidding, man? If Jenna has any sense, she ain't coming within a mile of your home, never mind your bed," Trigger huffed.

"Doc? I have no idea what you're talking about," he dodged.

Trigger snorted. "Yeah, right."

"Havoc, a little help, here?"

The man opened his mouth to deliver the magic bed commandment, just as the tangos woke the hell up.

Trigger sprang to his feet and raised his weapon. "Shots fired."

"No shit." Storm agreed. Three days they had been waiting. Now, so close to having his bed problem figured, the devil came out to play. They had it covered. One army ranger, a navy seal, a royal marine, and yours truly, ex delta. Time to put this sucker to bed. Storm grinned.

Two women, swamped in dark fabric, raving in Somali, raced at them. Mind-boggling, the way they moved so fast with all that material flapping around their legs. "What the fuck are they saying?"

"Death to the Infidel, sound right?" Havoc drawled.

Without breaking pace, the women hauled firearms from under their jilbabs. "Fuck me." Storm's gut clenched. Breathing deep, he raised his weapon and cushioned his finger against the trigger. *Ready.*

Sentinel's Bravo Team were experts in all weapons. Personally, he preferred hand-to-hand combat over noisy shit. And death lost its shock early in his military career, though killing women sucked big time. It shouldn't. Gender didn't discriminate, and the dark gaze of these zealots in a dress meant they wouldn't hesitate to end his sorry ass.

Havoc yelled for them to drop their weapons, but they kept right on coming. Given no choice, Trig roared into his head mic. "Winter."

Two pops in quick succession. The women hit the dirt. Their sniper had taken the shot and absolved Storm of the responsibility. It sucked. A crazy gift. Later, over a cool one, he'd thank his brother.

"Storm, with me. Winter, Havoc, circle round back." Trigger hollered. He added the hand signal they all recognized as he hurdled over the rear of the truck and tore ahead. Trusting his team to follow.

Storm braced his hand on the tire hub and vaulted after him. Head on a swivel, he scanned for shooters hidden in houses on either side of the narrow road. Sunlight sparkled off the muzzle of an AK-47, nosing its way from a window to his left.

"Your nine o'clock," he yelled at Trig, who spun on his heel and fired. A bearded guy slumped over the ledge, twitched and gurgled one last time.

"Target down." Storm confirmed into his comms as a girl, four, five years old at most, came from nowhere, clutching her teddy bear. *Hell, no.* He angled his body, creating a block between her and a sniper's bullet. No one was killing a kid. He'd fucking die first.

Winter groaned. "Quit with the dance moves, Storm. She's not a threat."

Hugging the furry animal tight to her chest, the girl vanished behind the rear of a nearby truck. If the bear was a bomb, it traveled with her. Ahead, through the haze, he glimpsed Havoc's camo jacket slipping around the side of a building.

Trig slowed his pace, dodged right, and signaled for Storm to shift left.

As soon as they were in position, hell's doors gaped wide. A woman flew out of the hut, screaming, followed by an old man. His arm pinned a terrified boy to his thigh. Imprisoned, the kid's breath locked in his tiny chest as he wriggled and kicked, but his legs were too short to make contact.

Storm swiped at the sweat on his forehead. *Fuck me. How many kids are there?* The old guy, mad as hell, eyes gleaming with hate, raised his chin, and issued a challenge.

By what had to be divine intervention, the kid broke free. Not knowing if the fucker had a weapon, Storm watched as the boy made it safely into the woman's arms.

"It's okay. *Halkaan isaga tag,*" Havoc shouted, waving his arm at them. "Get out of here."

Clutching the kid, the woman disappeared behind the building.

"Heads up," Trigger warned.

A shot rang out and a sharp sting pierced Storm's ass. *What the...* He swung back to the old guy, who raised his weapon a second time. *No fucking way.* Storm fired, and with a grunt, pop hit the dirt.

Storm swiped his hand across his ass and stared at his palm, covered in blood. "You're kidding me." Pain crucified his ass and shot into his lower back. His right leg went numb.

"Son of a bitch." Trigger chuckled. "Lean on me. Winter, cover us."

"Roger that," Winter acknowledged.

Storm hopped alongside Trigger and together, Havoc at their six, they made it clear.

"Where's Hassan?" Havoc grumbled.

Storm's leg scraped in the dirt. "Fuck knows." All he wanted was a bed. Any bed.

Chapter Two

Embarrassed. Jenna cringed at her big toe above the water in the bubbling foot spa. Yep. She sighed. Too long between pedicures. Sam sat next to her, waving a bottle of nail polish.

Jenna peered at the label. "I've never heard of it."

"Oh, come on." Sam rolled her eyes. *Paint Every Town Red.* Color of the month.

"Nope. Sorry."

"And there's proof. We should do this the fuck more often." Sam stretched for the red wine on the small table beside her.

They clinked glasses. "Cheers."

"Fuck, yeah."

Jenna loved hanging out with Sam, envied her ability to swear and not give a damn who heard. Unfortunately, it still seemed like yesterday when her BFF saved her son after Baxter abducted him.

Tom nagged his mum to get out more, but she wasn't ready to leave him at home alone just yet. Her rebound relationship with Baxter almost got him killed. She felt guilty for being clingy, insisting he come straight to Sentinel from school, and completely neurotic for being afraid he would vanish. Never make it home.

No wonder he kept stuff from her. Protected her. It should be the other way round. When Snake and Sam asked her to join them in New York, she had jumped at the chance to start fresh, but Tom hated leaving his friends. Social media catchups didn't count.

Thank God he loved spending time with Sam. Spent most of his weekends helping her train her dogs. Free of mum's over-protectiveness.

"Fuck me, this is good," Sam groaned, her head resting against the huge massage chair.

Being pampered did feel amazing. Pushing her crap taste in men to the back of her mind, Jenna savored the peppery Merlot and thought of Storm. The prime reason she hadn't returned any of his messages after their scorching lip lock was simple. Dating was not in her future. Not that Storm was anything like Baxter. She sighed.

Sam winked at her. "Me plates are blowing me kisses, thanking me for sharing the love."

The girl clipping her cuticles quirked an eyebrow. Poor woman didn't have a clue what her friend meant. Born and bred Londoners, she and Sam grew up around cockney rhyming slang. *Plates of meat—feet.*

"We should make this a regular event. Once a week, during our lunch break," Jenna announced plonking her empty glass on the arm of her chair.

Sam cackled. "Hell, thinking of taking time off in the middle of the day is hilarious." Her leg shot into the air, spraying water over the side of the bath. "Oh, sorry, love. I'm ticklish," she apologized and thrust her foot into the water.

The girl smiled. Jenna nodded. "I think she gets it. So, you're sticking with your color choice?"

"I am." Sam shook the bottle of flame-colored polish sitting beside her. "You?"

"I'm going for *Blue Moon.*"

"Seriously? Thought you were pale pink all the way. What's up?"

"Nothing. I feel like a change."

"And I call bullshit."

Damn. She never could hide anything from Sam.

"Out with it. Take another sip of this god-awful wine and spill. Would it have anything to do with you and Storm sneaking off the other night?" Sam said, her eyebrows doing a jig.

"You noticed?" Her, and who else?

"Remember, I train search and rescue dogs. Scent training must rub off on me. What happened? Did lover boy get around to making his move?"

Jenna ducked her head. Her cheeks flushed. Storm's kiss had woken up her libido faster than a shot of tequila. "No, nothing like that. We kissed. No big deal. A peck," she lied as Sam's eyes narrowed. "He apologized." Her bad, but they hadn't spoken since. A real shame because Tom enjoyed his company.

Storm was a gentleman. Gorgeous. And, underneath the macho, alpha thing, all the Sentinel men had going on, she sensed a softer side. One she might enjoy getting to know better. If things were different. If Tom's dad, Rob, hadn't died and left her prone to hooking up with nut jobs like Baxter on the rebound.

"Come on Jenna. When the team returns, call him and clear the air."

"Yeah, you're right. Will do, mum." Not one of her prouder moments, ghosting the guy.

"By the way. Don't forget Mia's birthday bash. There will be dancing. Princess with Two Left Feet here plans on making a clomping idiot of herself, and I expect you to be there with me. Copy." Sam nudged her elbow.

"Copy. Will Linda be there?"

"Yes."

"Only she can be, er... moody."

"A bitch. I hear you."

Jenna hadn't forgotten the day she first met Sentinel's receptionist. One of Sam's bonding lunches with the girls. Maggie, Winter's fiancé, loved knitting, so they had stopped at a yarn store in the East Village. Linda had given her a hard time, blamed her for making them late for their reservation.

"Like it or not, as my darling husband insists, Linda is Sentinel family. We can handle all comers. Right? Besides, it will do you good. Cheer you up."

"I'll think about it." Crowds freaked her out, and aside from the odd glass, she stayed away from alcohol. After Rob's death, she'd lost herself in the bottle. An ugly time and one she regretted. She shuddered every time she remembered her son helping his mum up off the bathroom floor. "Jake, Tom's friend, has invited him to go skiing in Vermont that weekend."

"Perfect. I never knew the lad skied." Sam lifted her feet out of the water and placed them on either side of the footbath.

"Rob had him on skis as soon as he could walk. Heli skiing in New Zealand was their last trip together before he died. I won't sleep, but I can't say no. It's taken him almost a year to make friends." While he was gone, she'd make sure she took the long way home after work to avoid the liquor store.

Twenty minutes later, they were done. Jenna beamed at her revitalized feet.

Sam grinned. "They look great. Let's go. There's a new gelato shop opened midtown. I see a Rocky Road in our future."

"You're mad. It's forty degrees! Anyway, I should get back. I've a ton of work."

Sam pouted. "My treat."

"Okay. I could do with a sugar hit."

"Great."

Sam had just finished paying when, wouldn't you know it, in walked Linda?

"Hiya," Sam greeted her, but kept walking.

"Wait," Linda called after them.

They both turned. "Sorry, gotta run. Enjoy your pedicure." Sam said.

"Hell. You're joking. On my salary? This place is way too expensive for me, and I'd rather walk on hot coals than let anyone near my feet."

Jenna cringed. The woman was uber scary when she scowled.

"Hell? You got that right, Linda, and it's where I'll be heading if I'm not back by the time Snake is ready to leave. It's our first date night in six months. The boss is planning something mega, and I still need to shower and change."

Linda shrugged. "Snake sent me. Wants Jenna back, now."

Jenna had no idea what her squinty eyeball meant, but she shivered.

"Some sort of emergency."

"Rain check on the gelato." Sam winked.

“Sure.”

Chapter Three

"Bet you wish you bought that bed. Any bed." Trigger chortled.

Son of a bitch. "Shut the hell up." Storm tried not to wince at the prod in the ribs. His ass burned while his best mate sat in the plane seat next to him, giggling like a two-year-old.

"I got you, bro." Winter's deep voice hummed in tune to the plane's engine. "Our den has a great couch. Besides, Maggie wouldn't let me hear the end of it if I left you alone in your place without a bed. Injured and all. Thinking of you sleeping on the floor would break her big, soft heart."

Storm cleared his throat. A reflex whenever he saw the mellow glint in their eyes when his teammates mentioned their women. Except Trig. he had been married, but never spoke about his ex, which, if his divorce had been anything like his own, he understood.

"Or there's that hammock at mine," Havoc chimed in.

"Thanks, but no thanks." He remembered the faded rag battened to the fire escape outside the closet-sized apartment Havoc and Mia were renting while the builders finished their dream house in Westchester. Havoc's mom had had the sense to haul her grandson off, to stay with relatives in Florida.

Seatbelt on. The sign flickered above him.

"Passengers and cabin crew, please take your seats. We are expecting some turbulence as we commence our descent into JFK." The captain advised over the PA system.

Peachy. Anticipating a rocky ride, pain twisted its grip on his right hamstring and gnawed at his sitz bone.

"Use this," Trigger smirked and shoved his pillow into Storm's chest.

"Yeah, man. Have mine." Two more squishy squares, smelling of sleep and sweat, soared over his head.

"Fifty bucks says he pukes within the next ten," Winter added.

"Jeez, guys, you're all heart."

"Aw, don't be a pussy. Does your bum hurt?" Trigger snickered.

"This shit is bordering on harassment." Storm shifted ninety percent of his weight onto his left cheek and shoved the pillows under the other.

"Yeah. Allow the *arsehole* some peace." Trig swiped a mock tear from the corner of his eye.

Storm chuckled. None of his brothers pretended to give a fuck.

As the pilot took his sweet time landing the damn plane, he cursed every air pocket touch down. With a mega exhale that could have sent them airborne again, he scrambled to his feet, and claimed his gear from the overhead. Resting one elbow on the top of the seat in front of him, he willed the doors to open—fast.

The conversation turned serious as they exited the terminal and headed to the car park. To a man, they loathed failing. Especially when casualties were involved and the target wasn't apprehended. Shit happened.

Their mission had been FUBAR from start to finish, and the sight of the old guy, bleeding out from a massive chest wound, haunted him. Nothing made sense. Women, kids, geriatrics. And no Hassan.

"Car's up ahead," Winter motioned at the vehicle Linda had waiting for them in the lot.

Opening the door, Storm gingerly arranged himself on the back seat, leaving the others to load up and get them on their way. Havoc drove, smoothly navigating out of JFK, onto the Grand Central Parkway, and heading for the city.

The mother of a headache thumped behind his eyeballs. He didn't care if he owned a bed. A space on the floor to crash would do just fine.

He'd slept in worse places.

Up front, sitting next to Havoc, Trigger shoved his phone in the holder on the dash, placed it on speaker, and called the boss.

"Evening, gentlemen. Glad you made it home safe after your *assignment*." Snake's English accent made Storm's rear sound like royalty.

Ha, fucking ha. "Not you, too, boss."

"Storm, my friend. Jenna is standing by, waiting for you at Sentinel."

The idea of Jenna's hands on his ass sounded like perfect medicine, but she had answered none of his calls. Made it clear, she had no interest in any aspect of his anatomy. "Thanks, it's just a scratch. It's late. Tell Doc the guys will drop me off at Bellevue. Nothing a few stitches can't fix."

"No way." Trig objected.

"Way. I'm a big boy. I'll catch a cab home."

Winter sniggered and slapped Storm on the shoulder. "Man. Stop talking out your ass."

Havoc nodded in agreement.

Fucking bottom feeders.

"No argument, Storm." Snake insisted. "Might take hours to get you triaged and I need you up, and present in the office, asap."

The boss had a point. Saturday night, Bellevue emergency would be a nightmare full of druggies, knife wounds, and battered women.

His blood pressure kicked up a notch. According to Linda, the last man in Jenna's life had been handy with his fists. Their receptionist had a talent for ferreting out personal information. Lousy at keeping secrets.

"Jenna is more than capable, and she's seen more than a few hairy arses. Yours is nothing special. Trust me," said Snake.

"All due respect, Boss. How the heck would you know? My ass is…"

As one, all three of his teammates flashed him the palm and shook their heads. "Too much information?" he mouthed. *About fucking time.*

"Settled. The rest of you. My office. Over and out." Snake ended the call.

Relieved when they pulled up outside Sentinel HQ, Storm ran a hand over his face and sighed. Five minutes into the trip, his wound had started bleeding.

Jenna was stamping her feet on the sidewalk, arms wrapped around her middle. He shook his head. How long had she been waiting in the cold? Prepared to tell her to move into the warm, out of the wind, Storm opened his door. But before he could swivel onto his uninjured cheek, Jenna ducked, hooked her arm across his back, and did her best to haul all two-forty pounds of him out and onto the sidewalk. "Easy, Doc."

"Lean on me, hero. Let's get you inside."

Height wise Jenna struggled to make it to his shoulder, but she was strong for her size. Always kept her cool when the going got tough. Still, he was big, heavy, and he didn't want to hurt her. He leaned on his palm and pushed, not too hard. The last thing he wanted was to knock her over as he hauled his massive frame out of the back seat.

"Go ahead." Jenna nodded at the others. "Snake is in his office waiting for you. I'll take care of him."

Storm wrapped his arm tighter around Jenna's shoulder and pulled her closer. "Promises, promises."

"Like that is it soldier boy? Just how many pain meds have you taken?"

"Now that hurts, Doc. This ain't no pork chop soldier boy. This is prime Delta beef."

Jenna huffed. "Whatever you say."

"Okay, Jenna. I can see you have this covered. Catch you later with a sitrep, bud," Trig smirked.

His teammates headed for Snake's office. He hated missing the debrief, but being this close to Jenna, her thigh nudging his side as he limped along the corridor, more than made up for his disappointment.

My ass might be in trouble, but there ain't nothing wrong with my cock. Big fella loved the sway of her hips, twitched when her coffee brown eyes gazed at him from under those super long eyelashes. As far as he could tell, Jenna never used makeup, didn't need it. At work, she kept her thick, wavy hair pulled back in a no-nonsense ponytail.

A heart the size of Jupiter. The woman never stopped taking care of the Sentinel team, their families. Her son. Yeah, family. The word hung like a medal behind that field shirt stretched over her perfect breasts.

A few steaks short of her target weight. Storm would slap money on the table she didn't eat until after she'd made sure she fed Tom before he left for school.

"Take off your pants and lie on the bed," Jenna ordered as she pulled on her white coat.

"Yes, sir, ma'am." Spick and span professional. Her guard up—always. Storm cocked an eyebrow and undid the button on his jeans. Took his sweet time, enjoying the slow drop of her jaw as his zipper hit the last rung and his cock sprang free.

Okay, her giggle could have dampened his ego if her smile didn't light up his dark day. So, here he was, jeans at half mast, his dick aimed at the shy doc.

One elegantly shaped eyebrow arched and for a mistaken minute, he reckoned she might turn her back and give him privacy.

"Lie on your stomach."

"Right." He shucked the denim and did as she asked. Should he apologize for being a tease, making her blush? Wouldn't matter. His rock-hard attraction to her faced front and center.

If it hadn't been for his recent over-eager slip. The kiss. Jenna might have stuck around long enough for him to ask her out on a proper date. But after he lost count of how many unanswered messages he sent, apologizing, he stayed away. Unless she joined the team for a meeting, then he sat next to her. She smelled amazing, which made him say stupid shit.

Cool fingertips probed the edges of the bullet wound. He winced, screwed his face into a ball. Just a graze, but one he intended to milk as long as he could if it kept her delicate hands on him.

Storm lowered his eyelids, and instead of the pads of her fingers, he imagined her lips peppering his ass with kisses, licking the crease between his butt cheeks.

Her brown eyes turned black. Wow! Where had her brain gone? Bonus, if it had snuck into the same erotic zone as his.

With his cheek squished against a thin pillow, Storm pictured Jenna's sunny smile, the magnet that drew him to her, spreading across her face as she rode him into oblivion.

"You were lucky. All joking aside. Gunshot wounds to the gluteal region can have serious consequences, damage to your pubic bone, rectum, or your peritoneal and stomach area.”

“Okay, Doc. I get the picture.” The thought made him queasy. Had to be the drugs Havoc pumped into him on the plane.

“Right then. I’ll finish cleaning the wound and stitch you up. Send you home with antibiotics and something for your pain. If I didn’t value my breath, I’d say no PT for a week. At least.”

He twisted his chin over his shoulder. “You’re joking?”

“Dead serious. I assume you are up to date with your tetanus shots?”

Her palm rested at the base of his spine. Tender and... Nah. *The kiss, dumbass, that fucking boulder you rolled across that path.*

Yeah! Good thing too. He’d sworn off relationships after his ex, Christine, walked out on him. Never spent more than a single night with a woman. An unforgettable night. He made sure of that, but once the dawn crept through the blinds, no exchanging numbers or, “I’ll call you,” spilled from his lips.

“Storm?”

“Yeah?”

“Where did you go? I asked if you were okay with a local anesthetic. I can knock you out if you prefer. Earlier, you seemed to be in a lot of pain.” She winked.

Doc had his number, and then some. “No. Kill the numbing agent. Let’s get this over with so I can catch the end of the debrief.”

“Are you sure? A small prick.” She pointed to the tip of her pinkie. “Promise. This will stay between you and me, if that’s why you’re worried.”

“Oh, hilarious. Enough with the below my belt jokes. Trust me, Doc. I have no worries when it comes to any part of my anatomy. I just want out of here.” His tone was harsher than planned.

Way to go, Bozo. He could be mistaken, but he swore she flinched. Didn’t intend for that to happen. He saved his mean for the enemy.

“Okay, then. I’d give you something to bite on. Pity, I gave my last bone to George.”

Her spine straightened, the spark in her eyes returned. A survivor. He gnashed his teeth and bit the sheet beneath him, shaking his head like a rabid dog just to be rewarded with a smile as wide as the Hudson River.

Stunning. "Stab me, doc." *Right through my fucking heart.* "Why didn't you answer my calls?"

"Sorry. I've been busy. Let's catch up for breakfast one morning next week?" she offered.

"Sure. How's Tom going at school?"

"Great. Relax. This won't take long, then you're free to play with the boys. For the record, my boy misses you, too."

Chapter Four

Jenna ought to fix her full attention on treating Storm, but half her brain scrambled to find something to say to break the awkward atmosphere. He had every right to be peeved, considering she ghosted him.

The nervous ache in her stomach made her bite down and roll her lips as her fingers worked fast, cleaning the wound and finishing the stitches. "There. All done. You're free to go."

"Thanks."

"Careful. Here, let me help you." She offered her arm.

"No need. All good, Doc." Storm grinned and rolled onto his side and onto his feet.

An acrobatic feat that left her hand dangling mid-air as she admired his perfect arse limping toward the debrief room. The Sentinel War Room.

Jenna scooped the dirty sheet off her treatment bed, tossed it into the laundry hamper, put her instruments into the sterilizer, and scrubbed her hands. The rest could wait until morning.

Dead on her feet, she turned off the lights and headed for home. Outside the debrief room, she was surprised to see Storm leaning against the wall. When he winced, she rushed to his side, thinking maybe she had missed something or, more like it, he hadn't told her everything. "Hey, you okay?" She grabbed his elbow.

"They're gone," he grumbled.

"Where?" Priceless. The look on his face. Ever since she'd known him, vulnerable little boy, Storm was never far from the surface. He tried to hide his softer side behind cocky banter, but she was pretty sure even his teammates saw through him.

"O'Malley's." He waved his phone.

Unhappy the boys left without him. He cursed under his breath. Jenna smiled and stepped closer. Sweet, how he tried, seldom successfully, not to swear out loud in front of her. Jenna waited for him to decide what to do next.

"Car's out back. See you tomorrow, Doc."

She watched him leave. His body really was as impressive from the back as the front. Earlier, he'd gone for shock value when he lowered his pants and succeeded.

"'Night. Drive safe." Her smile fake, voice too bright, she turned off the rest of the lights. Maybe she should have offered to drive him, but she needed a couple hours of sleep before she faced another, no time for lunch, day.

Half way out the door, she remembered she still had on her bright blue clinic clogs. Two minutes later, she'd changed, punched in the security code, and finally made it out the door.

Round back, in the small lot where everyone parked their cars, the last person she expected to see slumped against the gate, head bowed, was Storm. She reached for his wrist. "How are you feeling? Truth, this time." His pulse was strong, a little fast, but no reason for concern. His gaze met hers the second she lowered his hand.

"Peachy," he grumbled.

Of course, how could she be so dumb? The team had arrived in a rental vehicle. Storm's Jeep was probably parked at his place. "Need a lift?"

"Nah. Thanks. I'll call a cab. Wouldn't want to put you out."

"You're not. Besides, I have a duty of care. I'd do the same for any of you." She tried to match his flat tone, but suspected she sounded more hurt than she would have liked.

Storm shook his head.

Stubborn man. "It's up to you, but we could stop at a pharmacy for painkillers and antibiotics. The sooner you take them, the better." She pressed the unlock on her key fob and turned toward the car. The clash of metal made her jump.

Behind her, Storm was on one knee beside the garbage can. "Come on, soldier boy. With me." Kneeling next to him, she brushed his hair to the side of his forehead. "How many fingers do you see?" She held three right in front of his face. His eyes crossed.

"I could get used to this, Doc. Your arm around my neck."

Jenna sighed. "No problem. Keep getting shot in the arse and refusing help, and you'll nail it."

"Okay, I'll come quietly." Storm tapped the tip of her nose with his finger, sending a pleasant warmth swirling around the base of her spine.

"Anyone ever tell you, you smell good."

Yes. You. Just before you kissed me. "Not lately. Now help me out here. I can't hold you up forever."

"Then, allow me."

Like a match to dry wood, Storm scooped her into his arms before she could drop her weight and resist. "Put me down. You will…"

"Hell. You have no idea. Let's go buy some drugs."

Her laughter assaulted the silent lot. The sense of calm she always felt whenever she was close to the big guy washed over her. So right, it had to be wrong.

Chapter Five

Three Weeks Later

*L*iquor *With A Twist.* The downtown bar. The only place for Mia's birthday drinks, according to Linda. Their self-anointed social secretary for the night. Guess she didn't want to risk any surprise pit stops at a wool shop. Jenna crossed her eyes and chuckled, winced when the female singer, draped over the grand piano, murdered another note.

Whoever designed the bar must have had a speakeasy, vintage vibe going on, except the heavy wood panels, velvet curtains covering the window, and the constant noise from the crowd was claustrophobic.

In her book, a perfect night involved furry slippers, scented candles, and chocolate, while watching the latest episode of her favorite sitcom. The type of evening she would be more than happy to share with Mia's birthday.

"Something happened?" Maggie said.

Out of nowhere, Winter's fiancé slung an arm over her shoulder with enough force to send her flying off her barstool. Dressed in jeans and an oversized sweater embroidered with tiny hearts and her glittery sneakers, she looked adorable, and young. If the bartender asked for an ID check, it wouldn't surprise her. Dabbing her puffy eyelids, she sighed. *Jesus. I must look a hundred years old.*

"But it's okay if you don't want to share. I get it."

Maggie nudged her again, but this time Jenna's hands were curled around the edge of the seat, preventing her from taking that tumble. Pity the others weren't willing to go along with her friend. They had no intention of quitting with the questions. Jenna and Storm—the evening's main event.

Insisting she had no clue what they were talking about only encouraged them. She swallowed several times, trying to calm her anxiety. Back-to-back tequila shots didn't help. Her gut rebelled as the acid lodged above her sternum made her nauseous.

Twice during the evening, she'd pushed through the sweaty bodies shuffling on the dance floor and headed for the sanctuary of the ladies' room. Sitting on the loo, she had closed her eyes and begged for courage.

How soon could she leave? Jenna loathed being the center of attention, happy to fade along with the paint on the wall. The less focus on her, the better. All conversation should circle around Mia. After all, she was the birthday girl.

But, no, they refused to give in until she cracked. Sam glared at her. A definite threat shining from her squinty eyes. Run again, and this time she would follow.

"Love those boots. Clever way to hide fat ankles," Linda mumbled in between crunching the ice in her drink.

Wow! Jenna struggled not to laugh in case the Queen of Back-Handed Compliments took offense. "Thanks. The online shopping demon possessed me." The others would think she'd lost it if she said Linda meant to be nice, that she had limited social skills. *God. I missed my calling. Should have been a shrink.*

These past few weeks, the downtown Women's Health Hub where she volunteered had been crazier than usual. Back at Sentinel, swamped with supervising the team's quarterly medical checks, Linda had pitched in and offered to drive Tom, and his friend Jake, to Port Authority so they could make their bus on time to Vermont. A bloody lifesaver.

"The boots were a must have as soon as the ad popped up in my social media feed," she ranted, relieved the conversation had shifted away from her non-existent love life. "The Cuban heel makes me look taller, but they would still be in the box if Sam and Mia hadn't nagged me to wear them."

"Those boots are something else. That's for sure. Would never have imagined our resident Brit as the foot-tapping cowgirl type." Maggie laughed and broke into an off-key version of a song Jenna remembered from years ago. Boots walking all over some poor guy.

Feeling a little light-headed, no doubt from that last tequila shot, Jenna raised her arms in the air and swayed to the music. With Tom away, she had an entire weekend to herself. *Relax.* Easier if the DJ lowered the volume a couple of decibels and eased back the base level.

"Wanna dance, sugar?"

The shower of hot air hitting the back of her neck made her shudder. A man stepped from behind her. Big, same as Storm, but his muscled chest, hovering over her breasts, didn't give off the same heart throb vibe. Must spend a lot of time at the gym, but she'd bet her last dollar his calves were puny. The type she avoided, like frizzy hair on a wet day.

"Not me. I've had one too many." Jenna waved her empty glass in his face. "Er, Linda? How about you?"

"No way. I need the restroom."

Terrific. Linda waltzed off before she could beg. "Mia?" she squeaked.

Havoc's wife placed a finger to her lips, almost taking out the tip of her nose, and squinted. "You're joking. If my husband caught me dancing with another man, well, let's just say he's the jealous type."

"I asked you. Not your friends," the arse with the projectile pecs grumbled.

Beer breath splattered across her eyelids as he had grabbed her thigh. Dark blue veins popped on the back of a hand covered in ink. Treating it like an irritating fly, she flicked it with her fingertip.

When he didn't take the hint, she shoved it hard, tossed her chin in the air and straight away regretted it. The room shifted, and she hiccupped. *Too much bloody tequila.* The twat grabbed her arm. No escape. Unless she wanted to fall off that barstool.

"Ouch. I said, no." This guy was getting on her nerves. Beside her, Sam bristled. "You don't want to mess with me. My friend here is ex-army." She hated causing a scene, but desperation and alcohol had her mouth moving too fast. His grip on her elbow tightened. "Let go of me."

"Aw, come on, sugar. Quit playing hard to get. I seen you batting those eyelashes at me from across the room. Let's dance."

Of all the... The arsehole hovered over her. The next thing Sam mumbled something about the calvary arriving right before he stumbled backwards.

"The lady is with me," Storm boomed, his voice turning heads.

Standing between her and the jerk, Storm's fingers curled around the guy's shirt. Nostrils flared, the hand at his side clenched into a fist.

Worried there might be a punch up, and as she was in no fit state to play medic on scene, she gripped the edge of the bar and wriggled between them. *Piggy-in-the-middle. Terrific.*

"You're late, love." She laid her palm on Storm's wrist, hoping he'd catch on and let go of arsehole's shirt. He didn't budge.

"Yeah, where were you, big guy?" Maggie chirped.

"Excuse us." This time she pushed her chest against Storm's forearm, half smiled when his jaw dropped. She interlaced her fingers with his and pulled. "Come on, baby. You know this is my favorite song."

"I do?" His deep voice hit her front and center.

"Yep." Her nod sent the room spinning on its axis again.

"Sure, hon. Anything you say." His tone said the opposite, but she'd deal with that later.

The warmth from his palm flowed into the small of her back as he led her onto the dance floor, calming her nerves and settling her stomach. Keeping her eyes glued to the floor, she let him guide her.

"He's gone. You can look up now," he whispered.

Relieved, she almost asked him to stay for that dance. Except he kept moving. "Where are we going?" she asked, mortified at the number of eyes following them as he strode through the crowd at a record pace.

"Driving you home."

"No." She dug her heels into the floor and stopped dead. "I can drive myself home. Thank you."

"Not happening. You've had too much to drink."

"Whoa, cowboy. Let's try this again. Hey, Storm. Fancy meeting you here."

"Cute. Where's Tom? Home alone?"

And what the hell was that supposed to mean? "Away. Vermont. Skiing with a friend." And why do you care? Jenna almost added. "If you bothered to call him, you'd know." Two could play cheap knocks.

"Been busy."

"I gathered. Like I said before. He misses you. How's your arse?"

"Fine. And I don't do guilt trips."

Hurt flared in the shadows of Storm's gray eyes. Such a softie for an alpha, and she was being a bitch. "Sorry. I let my mouth carry me away. I apologize. Thanks for helping me, but I'm sure that guy back there meant no harm. It's a bar. Us girls are used to pushy men."

"To hell with that, Jenna. You, no woman, should apologize for being harassed by an asshole, anytime, anywhere. And as for putting his goddam hands on you. He's lucky I didn't cut his fingers off and stuff them down his throat."

Surprised at the force of his tone, she flinched. "Okay. You're right. I am a little tipsy. Sorry."

"Stop. You English drive me nuts with the sorrys."

The corners of Storm's mouth lifted into the smile she'd missed these past few weeks. The spot below her belly tingled. "I should get home. Early start tomorrow." She glanced at her friends. "And I didn't drive. We came in cabs."

Storm followed her gaze and nodded. "My turn for the sorry shit. Should have known none of you would risk driving under the influence."

"S'okay, big guy. We all make mistakes." She trailed her fingers along his arm. "But I don't want to spoil their evening, so if your offer of a ride still stands?"

"Sure. Least I can do after you chauffeured me the other night. Come on." He folded her hand inside his and tugged her to the exit.

Jenna caught Sam's eye and dipped her forehead toward the door. A knowing smile spread wide across her BFF's face. Oh yeah, they all thought they knew what was happening. Hating to spoil their fun, Jenna waved and gave her the girl-speak smile for, I'll fill you in later.

Chapter Six

Storm opened the door, waited for Jenna to go through, and slipped in front of her to protect her from the gale thundering down the block. He reached behind him for her hand and captured air, as frigid as the vibe between them.

Linda warned him it was a girl's only event when she let it slip about Mia's birthday drinks, but Storm's protector side, laced with a heavy dose of curiosity, itched to see Jenna. Make sure she got home okay.

The constant push to make sure she and Tom were always safe had started the day he'd met her flight from the UK. She masked it well, and she would hate it if he even hinted at the fact, but there was always something so goddam vulnerable about her.

When he entered the bar, he half expected his team brothers to be sitting at a corner table, keeping a low profile, ready to run any unwanted attention their women might draw.

Jenna had one thing right. How much she had to drink this evening was none of his business, even if she struggled to walk straight in her sexy cowgirl boots. The Cuban heeled, ankle length leather, showed off her slim ankles and lithe, athletic legs to mouth-watering perfection.

On the way to his four-wheel drive, he shortened his stride and slowed his pace. He didn't want her to trip in those cute boots that gaped around her slender ankles and showed off her well-toned calves. Man, he was fucking obsessed.

Despite the cold, Noho teemed with people, revved for the next spot on their evening's playlist, braving the weather, finishing dinner, heading for one of the downtown jazz clubs.

He and Trig preferred the watering holes in the blocks between the East and West Village. Whiskey shots and the call of wild, wild women? Lately, the combo had lost its appeal. Getting old. Thirty-six felt like a hundred. These days he preferred kicking back in front of the tv with a couple of cool long necks, watching the sports channel.

Jenna gulped as an icy gust threatened to throw her into the path of a motorbike. Storm caught hold of her arm and dragged her across the street. "Where's your coat?"

"Don't give me that look. I haven't lost it. It's on the…" Jenna stamped her small foot.

He caught the first half, but the wind swallowed the rest.

"I'm not worried about you losing your goddam coat," he roared as they reached the sidewalk. "I am concerned you will be hypothermic before we get to the Jeep. Put this on." He undid the zipper and took off his jacket. Taking hold of her arm again, he slipped her hand into the sleeve.

"Er, thanks. But it's not that cold.

"Fine." *Shut the hell up before you say stuff you'll regret.* Goosebumps erupted on her pale skin. Lengthening his stride, he forced her to break into a jog. *That should warm you up.*

"How's your arse?" Jenna hiccupped.

Out of breath. The sight of her plump round breasts heaving against her shirt stopped him dead in the middle of the sidewalk. "My what?"

"Oops, sorry. *Ass!*"

The urge to take Jenna against the wall and show her how well his butt worked blew his fucking mind.

"I'm your doctor. As you, my patient, have failed to show for any of your sch, ske…"

He chuckled. The way she wrangled her twisting tongue had him wondering how well she'd work it around his dick. "Ss ke…" he teased.

"Stop that. You've kept none of your follow-up appointments. That concerns me."

Storm leaned in, tempted to take that sassy mouth and kiss her senseless. "My ass is peachy. Thanks for asking."

Jenna's knees buckled, and he circled her waist with his arm. "Hey, you okay?"

"You did not use the words arse and peachy in the same sentence?"

Her laugh was infectious. "Jesus, Jen, I thought you were gonna pass out on me."

"Not me. I'm no swooning wallflower. Come on. I'll race you."

Jenna took off before he could tighten his hold. "Wait. It's this way." Spinning like a top, she changed direction. Bending both knees, he got ready to block her, but she feigned left, right, then tore straight past him.

"I win. I win."

The wind gathered strands of her hair and scattered it across her high cheekbones as she bounced off his four-wheel drive. "Come here, champion, let me drink a toast from those sweet lips." With his hands on either side of her torso, he pinned her against his Jeep.

"Storm, please. I..." Jenna's fist planted in the center of his chest.

"Sure." Disappointed, he reached behind her, opened the door, and lifted her onto the passenger seat.

Storm slid into the driver's seat. Stopping once for a red light, he tore through the city to Jenna's boxy apartment in Queens. Neither of them said a word. As he pulled up outside, now seemed as good a time as any to apologize.

"I've got some leftovers and a beer if you feel like a midnight snack." Jenna said.

You could have knocked him over with a feather. "What kind?" he mumbled, his jaw still struggling to make it off the floor.

"Spareribs?" Hic. "Shh." She glanced over her shoulder and pressed the tip of her index finger against her lips.

Fucking adorable. "Okay, Betty Boop. I'm in." He chuckled.

Jenna nipped the edges of her skirt and made like she was lifting her ballgown off the stairs. Doc, after a drink, make that a few. He could get used to waking up beside this clown. Right now, he settled for chasing her into her building.

They hesitated in front of her apartment door. Given the last time, he'd been overly focused on getting her horizontal. Half expecting her to take back the invitation, he held onto the memory of those few seconds, her sexy moans ringing in his head. Had that life-altering kiss blown any chance of making it past first base?

From where he stood, he had a full view inside Jenna's boxy apartment. Not a bad part of Queens, and rents were off-the-Richter expensive in New York, no matter where you lived. She and Tom deserved better, bigger. He laid awake at night wondering if anyone slept on the couch.

If money was an issue, he could cover the cost of moving—no problem. Knowing she'd refuse, he never offered the loan. Pride, he understood. After all, he had it in spades.

"Hic."

Spell broken, Jenna crooked her finger and sashayed to the fridge.

"Come in. Told you. Nothing to offer except ribs, I'm afraid. At a pinch, I could rustle up a green salad."

Resting his hands on the back of one chair tucked against a small table, he winked. "Ribs are great. Can I help?"

"Nope. I've got it. Sit. Make yourself comfortable. There are plenty of cushions for your peachy backside. With a grin, the force of her arm swinging through spun her in a half circle.

Jenna giggled and stared at her feet. "Crikey. I swear this building is on a fault line. We're moving. Either that, or someone built a skateboard ramp in my kitchen. What do you think?"

"I'm pretty sure tequila slammers will do it to you every time."

"Oh, don't be such a misery, Storm. I know I've had a couple, but..."

He raised an eyebrow.

"Okay, booze police. Three, but it is Mia's birthday."

"Like I said. Quit with the sorrys."

She frowned at the fingers dancing in front of her face. "You're right. I drank one more tequila than was sensible."

And to hell with keeping his distance. Storm released the chair. Two strides and his body hemmed her against the fridge. "Stop, sweetheart. Hear me. You are perfect."

"Really?" Her eyes crossed.

"Scouts fucking honor." Storm traced the seam between her lips with the tip of his tongue.

"Batswarynoiceurvyoutosay," Jenna mumbled.

Wide brown eyes stared at him above their crushed lips. Their laughter bouncing off the walls of her closet apartment. "Girl, you wear me out."

"Mmm, where did I put the serviettes? Hic. Napkins."

Acting as though she hadn't felt his erection pressing against her pelvis, Jenna opened and shut drawers. "Kitchen towel will do," he offered.

"Brilliant. Plenty of the stuff in my house."

Giving up on the napkins, she placed the skillet on the stove top. He should invite them over, show her a better way to cook ribs. "How's Tom enjoying the snow?" he asked.

Banging the side of her tongs against the metal, she scanned the shelves, looking anywhere but at him. "Great. I think. Haven't heard from them."

"When did they leave?" He grabbed the salt and handed it to her.

"Thanks. Yesterday. They planned to ski all day, but I thought he might call before he left this morning."

"Best time of the year for serious powder. Being the weekend and all, he probably thought you'd enjoy sleeping in." She should. Jenna worked two jobs and never complained.

"Yeah, probably." Not convinced, she half smiled.

Despite the alcohol, she moved around her tiny kitchen with the grace of a dancer. *Jesus.* What he wouldn't give to wrap his arms around her slim waist and sway with her.

Maybe they could forget about the food she'd allow him to bend her over the countertop and slip right on into her. Curious at his low groan, she cocked her head to the side. Clearing his throat, Storm sat on the couch and pretended to check his messages.

Food cooked, ribs on the plate, Jenna placed them, along with a roll of paper towel, on the coffee table, and flopped into the spot next to him.

He picked up a rib and offered it to her. "Here. Eat. You'll feel better with some food in your stomach."

"You're going to hate me for saying this, but the smell is enough to kill my appetite. But you go ahead, and I'm sorry about before. I was a bitch."

"No worries." Pushing the offending ribs to the side, he reached for the tv remote. "Wanna watch a movie?"

"Sure. But first I should explain."

"No need."

"Yes. There is. I'll keep it short." She straightened her spine. "Since Rob died, I'd like to say I haven't been with anyone. Truth is…"

The need to touch her burned in his belly. "Jen. You don't owe me an explanation. Put my wanting to kiss you, every mouth-watering inch of you, down to my overactive libido. You are beautiful. Inside and out, and I want to know you better. See more of you."

Realizing that hadn't come out quite how he planned, he cleared his throat. "But if you're not interested…" Slowly, he raised her hands to his lips and kissed each fingertip. Her eyes glinted and his world turned bright.

Jenna snatched her hand away. "Please. Let me finish. I tried dating. A complete disaster. I'm sure you've heard all about Baxter. The maniac almost killed my son. My fault. Until I get my head sorted, I've decided not to be with anyone. To concentrate on making the best of our new home and concentrate on being a good mum." She waved her hand in front of her face and sniffed. "Damn."

"Hey. Easy. I don't know the full story," Storm lied. Tom had told him plenty when they hung out at the gym together, but he didn't want to betray the kid's confidence. "I understand. And from what I hear, you are a great mom." Their gazes locked.

"Thanks. I'm sure you've been told before, your kisses are wonderful, and if I ever change my mind about dating, you will be the first to know. Call me a grumpy drunk, but never a tease. For now, I'd love it if we could stay friends. Okay?"

"Sure. But I won't lie, Doc. You'll be as shocked as I was when I tell you, since the first day we met, I've wanted more from you than a lip smack." Jenna's breath hitched and her dark brown eyes darkened. If his jeans got any tighter, they'd rip. "I wouldn't force you to give, or do anything you don't want to, sweetheart. Never."

"Thanks." Her crooked smile made his heart swell.

Before he could add, count on me to be here if you decide to look my way, the tequila shots caught up with her. Keeping her eyes open became impossible and her head thunked against the back of the couch, glided sideways, and came to a halt, slumped against his shoulder.

Out cold. He wanted to gather her in his arms and carry her to the bed he could see through the crack in the door opposite. Except he didn't trust himself not to stretch out next to her and get lost in the rise and fall of that perfect chest. Cursing himself for being that better man, he pulled off her cowgirl boots, lifted her legs onto the couch, and eased a pillow under her head.

"You leaving?" She snuffled.

"I am. Sweet dreams, sweetheart." The place was a damn icebox. He didn't have the heart to claim his jacket, so he raised the zipper, kissed her forehead, and slipped into the night.

Shit, Storm, you got it bad.

Chapter Seven

I will never drink again. Jenna groaned, thumped the side of her head, trying to shake loose the headache from hell. Knowing the pain was self-inflicted made it worse.

Drawing in a deep breath, she flicked the shawl off her legs and squinted at her knees. After leaving the bar, everything was a blur, except for the memory of Storm's smoky gray eyes holding her gaze as his tongue traced her lips.

She straightened her legs and decided to worry about that later. Tom needed breakfast. Saturdays he played basketball with Jake or went cycling with Tina, the pretty girl he rode home with after school. Or was it Sunday?

Then it hit her. Tom was miles away, skiing in Vermont. She swiped her hand over her face and spotted the glass beside the sink. Water with one of those fizzy orange tablets should help her pull it together.

She threw her legs over the side of the sofa and immediately her stomach rocked and rolled as though she were on a boat. Leaning back, she took a moment. Disappointed with herself for not saying no to Sam and her damn tequila shots, she waited until the room stopped spinning.

What time was it, anyway? She glanced at her sports watch. Twelve-forty-two a.m. No wonder the morning light was streaming through the blinds, casting the usual shadow ladders on the floorboards.

Keeping her head as still as possible, Jenna shuffled until her backside molded around the edge of the sofa. Storm must have left when she fell asleep. Collapsed more like it. Probably for the best, or she may have begged him to stay the night. Too embarrassed to imagine where that might have led, she buried her face in her hands. Drinking past her limit belonged in the bin with the rest of her high school habits. She'd be sneaking behind the gym block for a puff next. Come to think about it, that wasn't such a bad idea.

After Rob had died, a bird tweet, a change in the wind, made her sob, and for ages, she seemed to see him every time she turned a corner. One day she had broken down in the street, mumbling, *keep it together, keep it together*. People stared as though she'd lost her mind. Sad, yes. Schizophrenic, no. A man had shoved a fiver in her hand. Insisted she get something to eat.

On cue, tears pricked her eyelids, and all the times she'd messed up in her life frocked up to join her on the pity couch. Sheer luck or blessed? Jenna couldn't decide which, but those close to her enjoyed short attention spans. Her husband, Tom, Sam, they didn't seem to notice when she glitched, or if they did, they never stayed mad at her for long.

Okay, Jenna, no more whining flashbacks until you drink at least two humongous glasses of water. On a forced exhale that made her stomach heave, she stumbled to the kitchen tap.

Her fingers gripped the edge of the sink and her chin dropped to her chest. Christ. *You did not ask Storm if you could just be friends?* A platonic relationship with the hot man who made her girly bits whimper every time she clapped eyes on him. Hah! She must be mad.

Poor guy deserved way better. Why he bothered with her was a mystery. Nothing could destroy what she and Rob shared, but mourning her husband didn't stop her from being horny. Storm's confident swagger showed his arse off in the best possible way. A lopsided quirk of his full, juicy lips, and her panties were wet.

Even if she stayed celibate for the rest of her life, nothing would take away cravings for soft cuddles. Or the memory of how good life felt after passionate monkey sex while the moon cast shadows over the curve of a lover's thigh.

But Baxter almost killed Tom because she was weak. Surrendering to loneliness led to poor relationship choices. Jenna blew a strand of hair off her nose. Friends. Right. Self-imposed purgatory sucked.

Alone, at home, nursing a hangover, she had no problem admitting her secret, but no one needed to witness how pathetically needy she was once her workday ended and only the dark and the ghost of what should have been her life kept her company.

After several gulps of water, she felt almost human. A free weekend to do whatever. Were Sam and the other women in the mood for a movie or shopping?

Placing her glass on the countertop, Jenna staggered back to the couch and rescued her phone from the crack between the cushions. Midnight, but maybe someone was still awake.

Damn. A missed text from Tom. Several texts. Most likely calling to rave about the snow. Jenna clicked the first message.

Tom: *Hi mum. You okay?*

Jenna sniffed. *Gorgeous boy.*

Tom: *Don't worry.*

Don't worry? *Way to go, sweetheart.* She dropped onto the couch and stared at the word bombs that chilled any mother's blood. Boys loved their drama. Except cool was her son's middle name.

Tom: *Got sort of lost.*

How the hell can anyone be sort of lost? You either knew where you were, or you didn't.

Tom: *Battery low. Should be back soon. We're okay. I'll try you again when we get back to the resort.*

Trying to think straight while her head throbbed was impossible. The messages had been sent at seven p.m. Five hours ago. Dark. Freezing. And that was in her apartment. If they were outside in the snow... Too bad if Tom blasted her for being an uber mum, she called.

Hey, can't get to the phone right now. You know what to do. Leave a message. Her son sounded a million miles away.

"Tom, it's mum. Where are you? Please tell me you are drinking steaming hot cocoa in front of a log fire at the lodge, working up the courage to chat to a pretty girl. Normal teenage boy stuff, not missing in a blizzard. Call me, love. I'm worried."

Despite the choking suspicion he wouldn't answer, Jenna waited a few seconds for her phone to ring. When her worst fear proved true, she phoned Sam.

"Hi Jen, you still up? Are you at Storm's?"

Jenna caught Sam's, *I knew it,* tone and it might have been fun to share if she wasn't scared something dreadful had happened to Tom. "No. At mine. Alone. And before you ask why, I promise I'll catch you up, but it's not why I rang. Tom. He's missing. Oh, God, Sam, I don't know what to do."

"Hey, calm down. You sure? I bet he is..."

"Please, Sam." She did not need her to talk her off the ledge. "He sent me a text. Said not to worry, as if that was even a thing, and that he would let me know when they made it to the resort. He hasn't rung."

Tucking her cell under her ear, Jenna walked into the tiny bedroom, started pulling clothes from the closet they shared, and shoved them into her pack. "Just in case, I'm heading to the clinic to pick up supplies, just in case, then I'm driving to Vermont. Please tell Snake, and I'll call the Hub in the morning." *Ouch.* Jenna hissed. A prick from a dry cleaner's pin stopped her scared shitless rant.

"Okay, but phone the resort before you leave. It's possible they crashed as soon as they hit their room. Pizza the most important thing on their minds."

Not Tom. If he said he'd call her, he would. "I'll be in touch when I get there." Jenna disconnected and looked up the number for the resort.

"Good evening. Mountain Resort. This is Derek. How can I..."

"This is Doctor Fletcher. Please put me through to my son's room. Tom Fletcher and his friend Jake.

"Certainly. One second. Ringing for you, now."

While she waited, Jenna dragged her ski pants from a hanger and climbed into them. She grabbed thermals and a warm sweater, still hoping she'd hear Tom's sleepy voice, and she could crawl back to bed.

"I'm sorry, Doctor Fletcher, there's no answer. I will put you through to his voice mail and you can leave him a message?"

"No. Let me speak to the night manager."

"Certainly. One moment, please."

The line went dead. Had they lost the connection? Jenna raised her finger to call again when an unfamiliar male voice rumbled in her ear.

"Doctor Fletcher? Derek says you are looking for your son. Tom, is it? I'm sorry, but there is no answer in his room. If you are not comfortable leaving a voice message, I will have someone take him a note. Do you want us to wake him?" The night manager's tone dripped with condescension.

"No message. He went skiing this morning and never returned. My son called to say he and his friend were having problems finding their way back to the resort. In short, he's missing. Please call the Vermont Police, and local Search and Rescue. I am leaving Manhattan, now."

Without waiting for him to respond, Jenna disconnected and shoved her phone into the side pocket of her pack. As she pulled on her socks and boots and reached for her ski parka, a breath hooked under her sternum.

Chapter Eight

A slither of daylight eased through the bedroom blinds. Storm's eyes itched and burned, and some goddam jackass had him on speed dial. "Fuck off," he roared, and smashed his face into his pillow.

Hands down, it was Trig. His friend's nocturnal gym sessions had been a regular thing ever since he'd known him. The man pressed heavier than anyone on the team, but never stopped trying to shove the fucking weight off his chest.

Probably needed a spotter. How was his bud supposed to guess he needed sleep? As soon as he'd got home, he'd jumped in the cold shower. Unimpressed, still fully erect, his rock-hard cock couldn't let go of the idea of being balls deep inside Jenna.

The phone vibrated on the nightstand. Storm grabbed his pillow and hurled it across the room. Reaching out, he fumbled for his bleating cell. "You better be fucking choking under that barbell, dickhead," he grunted.

"Watch your mouth, Mathias Storm."

"Jeez. Sam?" He hated his Christian name. When it fell from his mom's lips, trouble followed. Like a teenager caught jerking off, Storm rolled onto his back and crossed his legs.

"Get your sorry arse to Sentinel. Quick sticks. Jenna needs you." Sam hung up.

Cryptic much. "Will do, Mary Poppins," he huffed. Interest piqued, more than a little concerned, he rolled out of bed. Half an hour later, showered and dressed, he marched into work and headed for Jenna's clinic.

Her back to him, reaching for a box of bandages on the top shelf, she didn't hear him enter. He had the ninja creep down to an art. Walking light ensured he slit the enemy's throat before they sliced his. Not wanting to scare her, he hung in the doorway. "Evening, Doc."

Jenna turned, but no smile. The one that brought out the dimples in her pretty cheeks. Pale cheeks. A tear sat in the corner of her eye. Taking two steps forward, another back, he danced in front of her. "How's the head?" he asked and raised an eyebrow.

Jenna shoved a box of antiseptic wipes into her pack. "Fantastic."

No way was that true. Often, when Doc shut down a conversation, he didn't push, but lack of sleep made him irritable, and in no mood to wait for her to come round. Holding her gaze, he tapped his forehead. "How's the head?" he repeated.

Like I said, "Fantastic."

"Ah, ha. So, that tear..." The tip of his pinkie pressed the corner of his eye. "It's the happy sort? Ace. Wanna share? I could do with a laugh." If that chin of hers got any higher, her neck would snap.

Her breath hitched. "You win, super sleuth. Have it your way. I'm not okay."

Storm eased closer. Jenna never admitted weakness. Never showed vulnerability. Giving in this easy, blurting the truth, scared his shit sideways. "Sam called. Told me to get my ass here pronto. Wanna tell me why?" It took every ounce of control not to take an extra step, pull her into his arms. Made sure she believed him when he said he'd move heaven and hell to fix whatever made her cry.

"Great. I should have known phoning her would push Sentinel's button."

Jenna's stool wobbled as she slapped the seat. He wanted to grab her hand and offer the furniture a break, touch any part of her she'd allow and share his strength, but he shifted sideways and gave her space.

"It's Tom. He's missing. No one's seen him at the ski resort for almost twenty-four hours."

His insides rolled with the hit, and he was done with the distance. Two strides and he snared her wrist and circled Jenna to the front of her stool. "Sit. What makes you so sure he isn't sound asleep, oblivious?" Dumb question. Doc was too level-headed to go off on a tangent and make shit up.

"He promised to call last night, but as you know, I was, well, out of it. Couldn't keep my eyes open. Before you left, did my landline ring?

Christ, he would have given an arm to say yes, Put Jenna's mind at rest. "No. I'd have woken you."

"Thought so. Sorry. Why did you leave? Something urgent?"

"Nope. Had stuff to do."

"In the middle of the night? No, don't answer. It doesn't matter, just not sure what woke me. Maybe I heard the front door close? Who knows, but I couldn't get back to sleep, so I checked my phone. There were several messages. All from Tom. Said they got lost, and he would call when he got back to the resort."

Storm squeezed the slim, ice-cold fingers in his palm. "You know teenagers." He'd been one once. That made him an expert, right? Allowed him to shake his head like a fucking grandfather. "A double shot of Jack's on an empty stomach, and they've crashed."

"You and Sam agree. The age of freedom and zip responsibility."

Jenna's intended laugh sobbed out of her. She clutched her throat with her free hand as though she could stop more tears from making it to her eyeballs.

"I get it. I'm over-protective. But, if anything's happened to him, I..."

"Hey." Storm cupped the back of her neck, tilted her toward him, and kissed the top of her head. A pathetic peck, when he wanted to wave his wand, and magic her pain into the ether. He nodded at her cell lying on her desk. "Take a deep breath and try him again?"

"Yeah, you're right. I'm overreacting." She picked up her phone.

"I didn't say that."

"True. I did. But it's true."

They listened to her call wiz straight to Tom's voice mail.

You know what to do. Leave a message.

Any remaining color leeched from Jenna's face. Storm slipped his hand from her neck to the small of her back and drew her to him until their foreheads touched. "Come on, we'll stop by mine, grab a bag, then go find your boy."

***

Storm sprinted upstairs to his bedroom, jammed ski gear into his duffel, and hurried into the adjoining bathroom for his comb, shaver, and toothbrush. In another bag, he made sure he had comms. Unlikely, they would need them, but he chucked in rope and carabiners, in case Tom had fallen and he had to rappel.

Lastly, he removed his handgun from the drawer of his nightstand. Used to leaving at a moment's notice, he was ready to roll in under ten. Jenna stood at the foot of his stairs, tracking him as ran down to meet her.

"Oh, God, Storm. Tom and Jake could be anywhere? What if they had an accident, and one of them is injured?" Jenna asked.

His insides lurched with the need to ditch the let's be friends bull crap and fold her in his arms. He opened the closet beside the front door, and as if they were going on fucking vacation, asked, "You pack a warm coat, hat, thermals?" That earned him a rapid tap of her foot.

"It's not like I haven't done this before, Storm."

He deserved her irritation. After all, both she and Sam were no strangers to wilderness rescue in the UK. Ticking off a mental list, his gaze traveled from her head to her feet. "Where's your boots?"

"Packed."

"When we get to the car, put them on. Save time when we arrive."

Jenna nodded.

"In the kitchen cabinets, there are snacks. Grab some for the trip," he rambled. To distract her, stop her from falling off the edge of her world.

It worked. Her eyes sparkled. "Tom loves Hershey's Kisses. Do you have any?" Her next breath shifted to a moan.

For a sec, he thought she might lose it. "Shit, yeah. Cabinet over the fridge. Grab them, and let's go."

"Yes. Sorry. I'll be quick."

"Remember. Eighty-six the apologies," he ordered as Jenna brushed past him.

Seated in his vehicle, Storm punched coordinates into his GPS and headed uptown to join the Taconic. This time of night, even if they didn't hit treacherous conditions closer to the snow, they wouldn't be there much under five hours. An eternity to a mom going out of her mind, thinking of her missing kid.

Above the drone of the engine, he could hear the what ifs shifting gears in Jenna's brain. "Sit back. Try to get some shut eye. I'll ring Snake and alert him to what's happening. Okay?" He patted her knee.

"Sam will have told him." Jenna's fingers curled around his. "But go ahead, make the call."

"Storm. What can I do for you?" Snake asked.

George barked once in the background. *Hi buddy.* "Checking in. Letting you know I'm on my way to Vermont with Doc. Take me off the roster for a few days."

"Guessing this has to do with Tom going AWOL. Sam said she rang you to check on her."

"Yeah. Could be nothing." Jenna snatched her hand from his. "But Tom's up there skiing with a friend. He messaged, said he was lost. Hasn't checked in since. We should be there in a few hours." They both knew how long it took to drive, but he mentioned it, as if putting it out there confirmed his commitment to the journey.

"Roger that. Keep me posted. We're here if you need us."

Jenna flinched.

Chapter Nine

The world looked like an impressionist painting, colors smashing into each other as they whooshed past the car window. Tense, her thoughts spiraling with images she failed to block, Jenna wished the Jeep had wings. Was Tom hurt, out in the snow, freezing to death? Had he lost his phone, or worse? *Call me.*

Huge gray clouds hung over the motorway. The air felt thick and more difficult to breathe with every mile they traveled. Afraid she might hyperventilate if her breath didn't find a normal rhythm, she focused on the number plates of the cars in front of them.

Occasionally Storm glanced at her, but she didn't dare look into his smoky gray eyes or reach for him. If one of his concerned smiles hit its target, she might blub all over him.

Stay positive. Keep it together. The words merged into a silent chant. They would find Tom and Jake. Alive. Unhurt. Nothing else was possible. Her son would give her the hug of his life before she hid somewhere and bawled for days.

"Hang in there." Storm's large hand slid across the console and covered her jittery knee.

The strong, callused fingers gently stroking her thigh soothed her, gave her strength. Grateful he didn't try to reassure her with empty platitudes, she allowed the warmth of the kindest man she had ever met to soak into her bones. "Thanks for coming." The few words were all she had as her breath shivered through her, and her heart skipped every second beat.

"You cold? Need more heat?" he asked, reaching to up the temperature.

"No. All good." A miracle he offered to come with her, considering she'd done nothing but push him away since they kissed. Storm kept hold of her hand as she sank deeper into her seat.

"Just listening to you think is wearing me out. Rest. Try to sleep," he insisted. "We have a couple hours' drive before we get to Killington. Once we reach the resort, you'll need your energy."

Salty tears stung her eyes, the same way they had the day she sat with Rob in the hospital and heard the oncologist tell him he had three, six months at best, to live. She wouldn't survive if she lost Tom.

As night blanketed the horizon, silence fell with it. The roads were icy, treacherous, but Storm's hand only let hers when he needed to steer them safely through a rough patch.

Too many hours later, they arrived. Her half-in, half-out nap had only made her brain fog worse. She rubbed her eyes and peered into the darkness cloaking the alpine resort. Tall lamps dotting the path to Reception bounced off patches of black ice.

While she worked at persuading her weary, still a little hung over, body to haul itself out into the cold, Storm went around back to gather their gear, then open her door.

The wind had a vicious bite, gnawing at exposed skin, stealing her breath, sucking the moisture from her lips as Storm helped her out of the four-wheel drive. Smoke spiraled from the chimney. A mix of something sweet, birch? And probably oak burning in the resort's fireplace. She loved the smell of an open fire. She closed her eyes, willing herself, a couple of hours on, to be seated in front of it, her fingers warming around a hot cocoa.

"Inside. We'll get you something to eat while I find out what's happening." Storm nodded at the entrance and signaled for her to go ahead of him. "I have an old military buddy who lives close by. She can help."

"She?" Kidding herself it had to be the bitter wind that made her voice rise an octave Jenna pasted on her poker face while he did a poor job of hiding his chuckle.

"A friend." He reassured her.

What? Did he suspect she was jealous? No way. Curious. Dying to know more about his female *buddy.* "You drove. Why don't you get something to eat while I check what's going on? I shouldn't have dragged you here. Tom is going to hate me when he finds out mother hen is crowding his weekend."

"He better not. Or we will have words."

Her gut clenched when he winked. How the heck could he stay positive? Part of her loved the way he stayed positive, cared. The other part loathed how he made her imagine more. Having him as a friend meant everything. Anything else belonged in the no-go zone.

Storm opened the door and ushered her inside before the wind slammed it shut. A bald man with huge ears stood on the other side of the front desk. His black jacket clung to his shoulders and the button in the center strained over his prominent chest. *Charles.* Said the gold nametag pinned to his lapel.

"Good evening. I'm Doctor Fletcher. This is...Storm." Thinking he might fill in the gap and offer his first name, she cocked her head to the side.

"Yes. Good evening. I'm the resort manager. Your boss, er, Mr. Snake." His gaze flicked to Storm before a sniff whistled through his nostrils. "He called. Said you were on the way."

So, this wasn't the guy she'd spoken to earlier. "My son. Tom. Have you heard from him?"

Charles drew in a breath, no doubt about to say words she didn't want to hear.

"I'm sorry, Doctor Fletcher. The boys have not returned. As you requested, we alerted the Vermont Police and our Mountain Search and Rescue. Accompanied by staff members and local volunteers, they have begun a search."

"Check your phone." Storm nudged her elbow.

Jenna pulled it from her coat pocket and shook her head. No message. The bones in her legs turned to liquid.

"With me." Storm led her to one of the foyer chairs and kneeled in front of her.

Jenna cupped his face and stared into dove gray eyes shrouded with concern. "I'm fine."

He leaned forward. His warm, wet breath drifting across her cheeks. Certain he planned to kiss her, she laid her palm on his chest, ready to push him away, and felt his strong, steady heartbeat under her fingers.

"Thought this might help." Charles handed her a large glass of water.

"Thanks." They said together.

Storm cleared his throat, and with a smile that didn't reach his eyes, he guided the glass closer to her mouth. "Drink, while I make a call."

***

His hand trembled. Another second and he would have kissed her. Kept on kissing her. Shredded his promise. *Platonic. What a load of…* He knew it. Jenna knew it. He'd bet his life on it, but if Doc wanted slow—he'd be a fucking snail.

He punched in Hawke's number for a video call. As the screen shot to life, he tilted it so they could both see the tech geek. A snake tattoo curled along the right side of her neck and headed between the cleavage, gracing the edge of the sheet tucked around her. Overflowing with scary intelligence, her black eyes took up two-thirds of her face.

"Storm? Long time, bud. I told someone the other day you were dead." Hawke smirked.

"Sorry to disappoint." The sheet beside Hawke twitched and a mop of blond hair flowed over the top.

"Easy, lover. Go back to sleep." Hawke shrugged.

Storm grinned. "Er. Sorry. Didn't mean to interrupt. Need a favor."

"All ears. *Diga mei, chico.* What can I do for you?"

"Got a situation. One of our team. Our medic…"

"Is she pretty?" Hawke asked, a grin lacing her voice.

"Not particularly." Jenna interrupted. The sides of her mouth twitching, despite her efforts to keep a straight face.

"Oh. *Perdón.* Just kidding, I'm distracted. Got my hands full, with this little hump right here." Hawke patted the mound next to her.

"This is Jenna." He pulled her closer. Any excuse to touch her. "Her teenage son, Tom, and his friend, Jake, are AWOL somewhere on the mountain. His cell last pinged at twenty-three hundred yesterday. Nothing since. Think you can find them, fast?"

"I hear you. Colder than a witch's tit out there. Text me his number. Give me fifteen, and I'll call you."

"'Preciate it"

The screen went dark. Across from him, Jenna paced. A waste of time encouraging her to sit back down, so he let her get on with it, prepared to catch her if she stumbled.

"Can she, Hawke, find them?" she asked.

"Sure thing. Want something to eat while we wait for her to get back to us?"

"No. And stop asking if I want food." Jenna threw her arms wide.

Exasperated. Edgy. The woman was fucking terrified. He hated it. Food equaled the last thing on her mind. Then her eyes watered, and Storm detested that more. Jenna swallowed her tears, and he wanted to shake the planet, make it beg her forgiveness for making her sad.

"I'm ready. And as for food, if Search and Rescue run ops the way we do in the UK, there will be snacks."

Water bottles topped up, he pushed open the door just as Hawke rang and Sam appeared. "Yeah. What you got?" he asked his tech hound. In front of him, Jenna hugged her friend. "Sam? Why are you here?" Jenna may be small, but she had a hell of a bear hug. Illuminated by the single bare light above them, Snake's wife, her dog, George, by her side, grinned.

"And that is a fucking dumb question, lovely. You didn't think I'd let you two go off without me and my partner at your six?" She scratched George behind the ears.

Storm chuckled.

"Gather you can't talk? Wanna get back to me?" Hawke asked.

"No. Sorry. Go ahead."

"Nothing concrete to report. I'm sending you a possible location. Will call when I have more."

"Roger that." He slipped his phone into the inside pocket of his parka.

"Thanks for coming, Sam. I know how busy you are, what with the new litter of pups, along with everything else."

It fucking baffled him why Jenna had such a hard time believing people cared about her. Especially as she never blinked when others needed help. Sentinel, the Women's Health Hub. Everyone respected the hell out of her.

"You guys go on ahead. Me and the boys will check things out here. If we find anything helpful, I'll call." Sam signaled for the dogs to follow as she headed inside the resort.

Storm touched Jenna's shoulder as she kicked twigs poking out of the snow. He was worried. She hadn't stopped trembling since they left Manhattan. "We won't stop until we find them, Doc." Until she had her son wrapped in one of his mother's killer hugs.

The dim, watery light of the new moon hovering above the trees made it harder to track, but no real challenge for his skills. Wind ripped through the tree branches hanging over the narrow path, turning Jenna's cheeks a cock-stirring pink for all the wrong fucking reasons.

Chapter Ten

Snowflakes stuck to Jenna's eyelashes as she looked in awe at the mountains towering around her. Way bigger than any hill on the English moors. Treacherous and deadly.

Doubting she'd ever feel warm again, Jenna stamped her feet and blew on the tips of her gloves. Frigid air zithered through her and settled at the base of her spine. But the howling wind wasn't the only thing giving her the shivers. Night owned the shadows when souls went missing.

Exposed too long in arctic conditions, Tom and Jake ran the risk of being hypothermic by the time they found them. Nursing her fear, she walked over to the group standing near an emergency vehicle and several ski mobiles and tapped the one who looked like the team leader on the shoulder.

The big man spun to face her and glanced at his clipboard. "Evening. Doctor Fletcher? Tom's mom, right? I'm Jim Peterson. Glad you could join us. Chuck, the guy at Reception, mentioned you're a medic. Let's hope we don't have to call on your expertise."

Without giving her a chance to confirm or respond, Pete returned his attention to the group.

"Listen up everyone, the temperature is dropping, and more snow is on the way." His voice boomed beyond the trees.

Jenna rolled her eyes. Anybody seeing the dim sky must know fighting for a deck chair by the pool hadn't made it to the agenda. Eager to get on with the search, she bit the inside of her cheek and bent to check her bootlaces. Her smart mouth wouldn't help find the boys.

"You, okay?" Storm caught her elbow and tugged her upright.

His solid frame shielded her from the head wind. "Cold?" she muttered as heat from his gloved palms glided over her hips and torso. A comforting heat blossomed in her bones, leveraging her hope and giving her energy. "Let's get moving." A sob away from asking for a hug, Jenna lifted her flashlight and shone it over the group, fanning out ahead of them.

"Okay, then." He tugged the zipper on her jacket that last quarter inch to her chin and brushed his lips across her forehead. Not a kiss, an inside voice insisted, reminding her not to lay her cheek against his chest and inhale his musky, male scent.

"That's it. Snug as that bug in a rug. Lead on." Storm winked at her, determination shimmering in his steel-gray eyes.

Tempted to the core to fall into the peace of his gaze, Jenna sucked in a breath and dodged in front. "Thanks."

"Pleasure." Storm grinned.

Cocky sod. Christ, she wanted to say things, feel stuff with this man. Add that to missing what she couldn't have, and her crappy day got a ton worse.

As they followed the others, she pictured her son's cheeks turning warm pink as he and Jake sat by the fire. Motivation to keep her heart beating. Ahead, a man from the group chatted with the woman walking beside him. Apparently, the volunteers who had been searching earlier in the day had called it a night. Too cold, poor light. Dangerous. Gone home to hot food and a warm bed. Sounded perfect, but she didn't care if she ended up being the only one still out there, she wouldn't stop until they found the boys.

***

J enna's nipples, stiff from the cold, pressed against her isotherm jacket. Could not lie, Storm appreciated the view. With respect, he cut his gaze to her profile, the outline of her high cheekbones, those honey brown eyes and pert nose. There would be blood if she bit her plush bottom lip any harder. Scared shitless. But admitting defeat, not an option as they trudged through the deepening snow.

Later. When Tom and Jake were found and tucked up for the night, he planned on asking her to reconsider this friend-only bull crap, and reckoned begging wasn't out of the question.

Still allowing Jenna to lead, he glanced at his chronometer. *Where the hell are you?* A couple of hours had passed since they left the resort and still no sign of the kids. Tom may be a teenager, but he was no fool. Before the two set off, he'd left word they planned to try one of the popular black runs. If that were the case, they should have spotted them by now.

The tree line disappeared into the blind-white landscape surrounding them. Any animal, visible in daylight, vanished into the haze. Circling overhead, two search and rescue helicopters kept them company while the sound of volunteers calling the boys' names echoed around them. If he didn't trust his inner compass, he'd swear they were walking in circles.

His boots crunched through the snow as he made a mental list of several teaching moments on Tom's horizon. Navigation by the stars, orientation. Survival at all costs.

Jenna stumbled. Catching her arm, he steadied her. Grinned when she cursed, her English accent made her sound like she was ordering afternoon tea. Dragging her legs through the icy damp that hit her mid-thigh, she kept right on truckin'.

His height gave him an advantage. Despite carrying the heaviest pack, even at its deepest, the snow never made it past his knees. "Hey. Wait up." Storm's pack slid from his shoulder and landed in the snow with a soft thud.

"No. We have to keep going," she muttered through the scarf covering her mouth.

Storm didn't move. "I need water." *So do you.*

"Sorry. Of course."

With the patience of a schoolteacher handling an over tired child, Jenna sighed and leaned against a tree.

"Here." Storm offered Doc his bottle.

"It's okay. Got some." She drew a flask out of her pack and waved it at him.

Mission accomplished.

"Damn. I forgot my watch. What time is it?"

"Not sure," he lied. They were losing the light and tagging how long the boys had been missing wouldn't help any. The beam from his headlamp picked up her breath, threading like smoke above her head.

Hands resting on her knees, her short pants worried him. Neither of them had eaten since the ribs last night. Two strides and before she could push him away, he cupped her cheeks and tilted her face until their eyes met. "Hang in there, Doc. We will find them. You have my word."

She leaned into his gloved palm. "Yes. You're right. Sorry."

Again with the apologies. He frowned and her answering grimace harbored pain, doubt. Guilt. An emotion he never indulged, but the idea he could fail her, that they may never find the boys, threatened to bring Storm to his knees. *Pull yourself together.* He did this shit for a living—brought people home.

Her hand pushed against the center of his chest, but he held on a breath longer. "I swear, Jenna." She must believe him. "We will find them."

Jenna nodded and sniffed. "Thanks for being here with me. You're a good friend. Not sure I could do this without you."

"Sure you could. Drink, rest a sec, while I check up ahead." Holding onto her upper arms, Storm propped her against the tree. Keeping her in his peripheral vision, he climbed several feet to higher ground. Off to his left, a couple of searchers strapped on snowshoes and took off back in the direction they came.

Storm removed his glove, adjusted the scope on his binos and panned the white curtain shrouding the mountain. Straining to hear more than the wind rushing through the trees, he sucked in a breath as if he could hold back the night.

At the bottom of the slope, a flicker, a shift in the branches, made his stomach clench. Storm adjusted the sights for a clearer view. Two solid stationary shapes. A short distance behind them, a larger mass moved slowly in their direction.

Storm swung his focus back to the two. *Yes.* What looked like the Sentinel, standard issue day pack he gave Tom to carry his gym gear, sat on the ground between them.

"Storm?" Jenna called out from below, wading through the snow, heading straight for him.

He shook his head, and she froze, her sharp pants punching the air. The way Jenna picked up on his signal made him wonder how responsive she'd be in bed. To his touch, exploring her skin, hair, every soft, pale inch of her. *For fuck's sake. Focus.*

He widened his stance, and with one eye glued to the solitary figure now hidden behind a tree, he stretched for Jenna's hand and hauled her to his side.

"Can you see them?" she asked.

The desperation in her voice hooked under his ribs and tugged hard. "Easy," he whispered, and brushed a strand of hair from the corner of her mouth.

"Where? Show me." She gripped his shirt.

Chapter Eleven

Tom swiped his dripping nose on his parka cuff. After their phones died last night, he and Jake agreed rather than walking in the dark, their best bet was to stay where they were and keep warm until daylight. He kicked himself for not packing a compass, but neither of them had imagined getting lost.

When he saw mum, he planned on thanking her for making him stick it out at boy scouts, especially as he'd resisted big time, mainly because the village hall where they met had zero heating. Last night, his Camping Merit Badge had got a workout.

He'd been chuffed when they erected a makeshift shelter out of branches and a tarp, lashed together with the rope he almost forgot to pack. Despite the heavy pounding from the wind, it held strong.

He smiled. Jake made him pinkie swear he would never tell how they spent the night in the same sleeping bag, locked in a bear hug to keep warm.

"I'm dead," Jake moaned.

"Shut. Up. We are not dead, and I don't plan on dying. Not today." Tom laughed. Not the happy, never wanted it to stop kind he shared with Tina. More of a snort that he regretted the minute his mate cringed. But negative thinking wouldn't help get them find their way back to the resort.

"Oh, shivers, bro. Your dad... he's dead. I mean... he's... I'm a dumbass."

Watch out, Mr. Sensitive woke up. "Nah. You're good. I miss him, that's all." Even when he got really sick, his dad never complained.

Jake nodded and became really interested in a single leaf sticking out of the snow. Tom squinted at the sky, cursing the weak moment when he called his mum. She'd be sick with worry.

In zero disability, working out the direction of the lodge proved impossible. As though the world had turned upside down and dangled them over the edge.

Shielding his eyes with the edge of his hand, he half hoped to see a rescue helicopter emerging from the clouds. He could swear one flew over earlier. The cold must be messing with his head.

Wind whistled through the denser trees, punctuating what his dad called igloo quiet. Unlike Jake, dad understood the space with no noise where feelings struggle to form words. They never used to speak much when they went fishing. Happy to hang. Except that last time when his father had made him swear to take care of mum. *You made a right mess of that one.* Tom shrugged off his pack and rummaged inside for food.

"You're my best friend, bro. It sucks I got us lost." Jake groaned.

"Nope. Not your fault. We should have ignored that dude and skied the run we planned." Now he thought about it. The dude came out of nowhere. If he'd stuck his arm out, he could have been a living signpost, pointing in any direction other than the legendary powder they'd been chasing. He practically dared them to follow his crud map. They were stupid to fall for it.

Tom sank the tip of his pole into the snow. Had to be at least three inches deeper than when they set out yesterday, and it didn't look like quitting in a hurry.

"Yeah. You say it wasn't my bad but try telling that to my mom."

Tom rubbed his palms together. Inside the insulated gloves, his fingers burned. "I hear you. Mine never said it, but it was my fault when everything went ballistic with Baxter. I should have stopped him..."

"Stop, dude. That guy was a crush-your-skull psychopath." Jake punched his fist into his palm.

Tom smiled. "Definitely a pyromaniac." He laughed. Proper this time.

Frigid air whistling in his windpipe. Never thought he'd say it, but a fire, right this minute, would be awesome.

***

Shep liked this Tom kid. What did they say in the movies? *If only I'd met you in another lifetime. Things might have been different.* Yeah. Nah. His life didn't include friendships. It revolved around money, pay checks. The alimony he paid every month to his bitch of a wife.

The five-figure fee for this kill would tide him over for a year, with or without a bonus for throwing in his whiny bitch friend. No worries. He planned on smiling all the way to the bank.

After they took off with his cracker box map, he'd followed them, listened to their shit while they trudged in circles. More painful on his ears than the cold gnawing his bones. Thinking about it, he should do the whiney one first. Before he slit his throat, he'd tell him his mother was a saint for not strangling him at birth. His constant belly aching must have driven the woman insane. Shep adjusted his goggles. They were so tight, his head throbbed.

"We are only living in New York because of me." Tom said with a shrug.

Jesus! Belly aching is contagious.

"Said *we* needed a fresh start, but mum meant me. *I* needed a fresh start. She was sick of copping my anger for breakfast, lunch, and dinner."

Whiner stretched for Tom's high five and missed by a mile. *Loser.* Good friends. Shep lowered his weapon. Too damn cold to wait much longer before finishing them off, but this pair intrigued him.

As a kid, he'd bounced from one foster shit hole to another, never got close to anyone. He laid awake nights wondering where that other road, the path he didn't travel, led.

If he let these boys live, where would they be in ten years? *Getting all philosophical, Shep. Must need a beer.* He got off on what if games, especially when he had the power to kill the dream. Any goddam place or time.

For sure, whiner would be an evil-shit dentist. Shep's jaw ached—long stretch between a drill and a rinse. He belched just thinking about the minty antiseptic mouthwash. Our buddy Tom? He stroked his chin. A lawyer. Hell, the way he handled his friend, he should be a vet. Kind to all fucking animals.

"Shit!" Whiner hopped sideways as a massive sheet of snow slid off the tree branch. Slivers of ice smashed into the sleeve of his super expensive ski jacket.

Pity the coat wouldn't fit him, but the kid's boots might. For a runt, he had humongous feet.

"No one will believe we were told to come this way. You know how much the fine is for straying outside of the resort's trail boundaries?" Tom shook his head.

"Nope." Whiner shrugged.

"Thousands."

"Seriously, dude?"

Oh, yeah, dipshit. Shep chuckled.

"Yep. We should never have listened to that arsehole."

True. *Didn't your mom tell you? Never talk to strangers.* Shep's grunt echoed through the trees.

"Hey, you hear that?"

Tom ducked and peered in his direction. Shep hauled his weapon onto his shoulder.

"What? The only thing I hear is my teeth chattering. Man, I can't feel my toes. Should have chucked extra socks in my pack," he grumbled.

The wind whistled an affirming, *copy that.*

"Here, have my spare." Tom sighed and tossed the socks at his friend. "Drink the last of the Gatorade, too. I'll throw up if I have any more."

"You, baby!" Deciding they both should be dentists, the words were out of his mouth before Shep could shut the fuck up.

"Dude. Tell me you heard that?" Tom said.

"Told ya. Can't hear nuthin' except my molars gnashing together."

"Over there. Through the trees."

Aw, shit. Tom pointed at him. *Stayed too long at the party, boyo.* The do-gooder volunteers had found them too. A couple of them perched on the ridge behind him.

He flipped the safety and aimed. *Inhale, one, two. Exhale, three, four. Fire!* The shot echoed through the brush and fuck him, it went wide. For a micro-second, like hunted deer, the boys were stunned before they scattered. Above him, the pair he'd spotted earlier crashed through the snow.

Chapter Twelve

"**N**o!" Jenna screamed, tore her arm from Storm's grip and slid down the slope. Low branches cracked under her weight and the ice bit into her palms as they tried to slow her descent.

Storm followed, yelling for her to stop, wait. *Go to hell.* If putting herself between whoever was shooting at Tom and Jake saved their lives—consider it done.

Her damn foot snagged a rock, hurling her forward. Out of control, arms flailing, air locked in her lungs. Storm's arm hooked her middle, jerking her hard against his torso. A split second later, his heavy, thick forearm pinned her to a tree.

"Don't move," he growled.

Storm's warm breath brushed her numb face. Beyond angry he'd try to keep her from Tom, she clenched her jaw, dragged her foot through the snow and aimed for his shin. "Get off me." With a jerk of his hips, he avoided contact.

"Stop." Elbows bent, palms up, he backed off an inch. "You want to get killed?"

"I don't care. I..." She watched Storm's jaw drop as fury fired in the depths of his smoky gray eyes. "Damn it." Forearms resting on her thighs, Jenna struggled to speak.

"Okay. Breathe. Grab my belt and stay behind me. Do not let go. We move together," he ordered.

Seeing the gun he pulled from his parka, Jenna appreciated America's second amendment. Ever-ready alpha at her service. Two hands clasping his firearm, Storm placed one foot in front of the other, graceful, sure-footed, the strength of his thighs steadying her, so she didn't fall and break a leg.

No more gunfire. No sound from Tom either. Christ, was he hit? As they rounded the next tree, heart thumping, Jenna lost her slim grip on control. "Tom!"

"Quiet." Storm hissed.

He swiveled to face her and suffocated her scream with his hand. Digging her fingernails deep into his wrist, she broke the seal. "Over here." Jenna raised her arms and waved them frantically in the air. If the gunman focused on her instead of Tom and Jake, they might escape. "Here, over..." Storm's massive torso slammed into her, bringing them to the ground.

"Move again, and I swear I will knock you out."

Flat on her back, gasping for air, Jenna's head jittered on her shoulders. His voice had a hard edge she'd never heard him use before. Not with her. She took a deep breath. Should she struggle? Why bother? No way could she shift him. "Okay," she spat the words, bile pooling in her throat.

"Christ, Jenna, you scare the hell out of me."

Storm hovered over her, his breath puffing against her cheeks, his gaze thunderous. A fierce protector. A deadly enemy. With a bloody erection if she wasn't mistaken. His eyes crinkled. Insufferable. Arrogant. Beautiful.

For Christ's sake! "Get off of me." At the threat of her knee endangering his crotch, he rolled onto his elbow, giving her space to flip and scramble to her feet.

Except for the sound of the wind dusting snow across the slope, nothing moved. Suspended in the eerie bubble, she could almost believe she imagined the gunfire. Her eyes burned. Damn it. Somewhere between being pinned against the tree and body slammed, she'd lost her goggles. Raising her hand to shield her eyes from the glare of the snow. Storm sprang to his feet.

"Here, take mine," Storm offered.

"No. You need them."

"I have a spare."

Of course. Jenna shook her head and flipped the headband over her finger. Over Storm's shoulder, something shifted. Tom's blue beanie, the one she bought him for the trip, bobbed through the trees.

"Mum." Tom hollered.

Yes. "Here, baby. I'm here."

Relief at seeing the boys rushing toward them buckled her knees. Not wanting to let another second pass before hugging her son, she turned to meet him halfway, but Storm gripped her wrist. The pistol in his other hand scanned a wide arc through the trees.

"Easy." Storm growled. "Person with a fucking gun."

Her blood turned molten. It irked that he had to remind her. Tom threw his arms around her and buried his head against her heart. "Tom Fletcher. Where the hell have you been?" She cradled his face between her palms and smothered him with kisses. "You are grounded for the rest of your life." Eyes for no one else, she forgot Jake until he moaned.

Like a well-worn habit, Storm had the situation under control. Stripping off his parka and wrapping it around the shivering teen.

"Mum. Get behind the tree. Didn't you hear those shots?"

Her attention swung back to her son and smiled. He and Storm had more in common than she wanted to admit. Sensible, practical. Traits she had in spades when she wasn't out of her mind worried for her son. "Thanks, Storm. For being here."

"Save it." His voice had softened, but not much. "We need to move. Now." Storm lifted his chin at the ridge.

With a nod, she angled Tom's shoulders back the way they had come. "Do as Storm asks. When you're safe, and I've examined you both, made sure you're okay, we'll talk."

"We aren't hurt. Honest. Just cold. A few cuts and bruises." Her son forced the words through gritted teeth.

"Exactly." Jenna swallowed the voice soaring to an octave above hysterical.

A few yards over the ridge, Jim Peterson and a handful of volunteers poured from the trees. During the past hour, the wind had picked up, gusting through the clearing, driving the snow in every direction. They needed shelter faster rather than sooner.

Peterson undid the top flap of his backpack, pulled out a couple of space blankets, and handed them to Jake and Tom.

"Thank you," she muttered, regretting her earlier arrogance.

"Did you hear the gunshots?" Tom asked him.

"Sure did, son. Damn hunters. Not the first time their aim has gone wide. Don't worry, none. Cops are on it."

"What's the quickest route to the resort?" Storm asked.

"Yeah. We're starving." Tom added through chattering teeth.

Teenagers. Boundless appetite. Jenna chuckled, her chest swelling with something other than her next breath. She glanced at Storm, praying they didn't have to retrace their steps, and he winked. Doing his best to make her feel better. And he did. Partners. Together, a part of her imagined they could do anything.

"I'd bet my poker winnings those hunters are long gone, so if you boys are up for a short walk, there are a couple of snowmobiles out on the road." Peterson half-turned and pointed to his left. "You could wait for the rescue truck to get here, but it's probably best to keep moving before we lose the daylight. Resort is several miles that way."

"Thanks. We'll head for the snowmobiles. Appreciate all your help." Storm shook the guy's hand. "You okay with that?" he asked, turning to face her.

Bit of a late ask, but she was too tired to make an unimportant point, so she nodded. Top priority, getting the boys somewhere dry and warm, far away from gun toting maniacs. *May their balls freeze off.*

Chapter Thirteen

"Move." Storm shouted. His tone harsher than he intended. Blame it on his lips. Numb from the bitter cold. A damn lie. Anger twisted the hell out of his gut and refused to fuck off.

Acid bile rose to his throat every time his brain replayed the image of Doc giving the finger to danger and bounding after Tom. Reckless. Fucking suicidal.

He got it. Jenna was a medic and a mom with protective instincts as strong as his own. When the stakes soared, the risk of losing the plot went beyond high. But bleeding out in the snow from a bullet wound to the head seldom achieved the objective.

Weapon at the ready, he scanned the trees on either side of them. Following the road was risky, especially with unarmed civilians. In his line of work, Storm had lost count of the extractions he and his teammates had executed, but they weren't around. He'd love a chance to get his hands on their attacker's neck, except it didn't look like the asshole planned on getting close.

A few steps ahead of him, Jenna pushed into the wind, her grit impressive. Her not-so-subtle eye roll at the team leader's bull crap earlier when he said hunters were to blame matched his instincts. *My ass.* Taking potshots at a couple of lost kids made no fucking sense.

Smaller and skinnier than Tom, his friend Jake walked in a not so straight line, struggling to keep up with Tom. His guess, the boys were a snowflake away from hypothermia. Potential, serious casualties if he didn't get them under a hot shower, stat. Storm lengthened his stride and pulled up alongside Jenna. "You reckon I should carry the kid?" He kept his voice low, so he didn't embarrass Jake.

Jenna shook her head, her ragged breaths colliding with the frosty air. Cold. Scared. Acknowledging her skill set, he checked in on the lingering dread whistling through the hairs on the back of his neck. "Okay. Let's step on it."

Doc's chin lifted, determination flowing off her in waves. He meant it when he said she scared the shit out of him. The unconditional way she protected the boys with everything in her.

Not on my watch. The military trained him to take the bullet. And seeing as he still planned on at least one more kiss before he died, taking a bullet from this mother fucker did not figure in his bigger picture.

Flushed from the cold, her cheeks aroused parts of his body that had no business offering an opinion. Kick his sorry ass, but he ached to fuck away her fear. After shock sex worked. His cock twitched.

Relief washed over him as the two snowmobiles Peterson mentioned rose like ghostly trojans up ahead. He fist bumped Jake, who managed a shaky grin, just before the Boo Demon saw his fucking chance.

Too busy lusting after Doc, he almost missed the glint of watery sunlight bouncing off metal in the trees. "Run." Storm roared.

A man dressed in snow camo raised his firearm and fired three shots before darting across their path and vanishing into the forest on the other side of the road. Storm listened for a cry or a body hitting the ground. The shots were wild.

Pale blue eyes, swimming with questions, found him. Jenna's gaze, brimming with terror, threatened to wrench his heart from his chest. He dabbed his mitten at the sleds. "Move. Stay low." Weapon raised Storm angled his body to where he last saw the shooter. *Show me an eyelash, fucker, and you're dead.*

"That one." He signaled Jen to take the snowmobile furthest from the threat.

"Jake. With me." The kid grunted. Knees bent, Storm gripped his Glock, lifted the boy onto the rear seat with his spare hand, then grabbed helmets from the cargo storage box.

One last look at the trees as he mounted and locked the key in the ignition. Jenna did the same. He assumed she could operate the snowmobile by the way she lowered the ice scratchers. His woman aced every fucking test.

While they waited the few seconds for the engine to reach temperature, Storm snatched off his glove and hit Sam's speed dial.

"Where are you?" she snapped, sounding as though he was late for dinner rather than running from a fucking lunatic.

"Approximately fourteen miles out from the lodge. Taking fire."

"On our way." George barked a loud *copy that*. The phone went dead.

He turned to Jenna. "Ready?" Spine ramrod straight. Her breath hitched. "You okay?" he hollered over the wind. God forbid he hurt her when he took her down earlier.

"Fine." She smiled and glanced over her shoulder at Tom. "Hang on, love."

Storm revved his engine and swerved into action. Snow sprayed across the windshield. With cargo more precious than any he had ever encountered on a mission under his protection, his stomach churned. As far as he could tell, they weren't followed.

Minutes later, a four-wheel-drive drove straight at them. One hand guiding the vehicle, he raised his weapon and almost sobbed with fucking joy. His fur buddy George, barking for all he was worth, came into sight, sat in the passenger seat next to Sam.

They screeched to a stop and dismounted. Storm half dragged, half carried Jake into the rear of Sam's truck. "Stay down." He shoved the kid's head onto his knees.

Weapon raised, dog by her side, Sam escorted Jenna and Tom to safety. "Stay down," he repeated, clearing the way for them to climb in beside Jake.

Sam hopped into the front passenger seat. "You drive." She tossed him the keys. "Up." George sprang onto her knee.

Engine running, Storm secured his belt.

"I'm cold." Jake groaned.

Storm checked his mirror. Something about the fear in the boy's eyes reminded him of Sentinel's last mission. The boy in Somalia was younger, but he'd never forget the terror on the kid's face when he turned the old man into chopped liver.

That day haunted him. One, because he still couldn't sit for long, and two, Hassan was still out there. "Hang on," Storm ordered. He shifted into second, rolled into the middle of the road, and gunned the heater. No reason for anyone to freeze to death.

"Can you see him, the man firing at us?" Jenna's voice trembled.

"No." Storm squinted at the side-view mirrors covered in sleet. Treacherous conditions, but he jammed his boot onto the accelerator and drove as fast as he dared.

Slush from the road sprayed the back windows. "Mum!" Tom cried.

"It's okay." Storm glanced at Jenna in his mirror. "Right?"

"Yeah." Doing her best to keep it together, she tossed him a smile that threatened to break his heart.

Folding her arms over the boys' heads, Jenna used her slim torso to shield their bodies.

"Lights up ahead." Sam said as they approached the resort.

Storm figured the shooter must have driven in the opposite direction, more concerned with getting away than chasing after them. He turned off the engine and hooked his forearm over the back of his seat. Watching Jenna's fingers stroking the hair from Tom's forehead, an enormous lump formed in his throat. "Everyone okay?" he croaked and nudged Jake's elbow. "All clear, bud. You can raise your head."

"He's gone." Jenna assured him.

Strawberry red, the end of her nose and cheeks, looked as though someone had pinched them hard for a week. Tom sniffed. Doc inched open her parka and slid a tissue from the inside pocket. Storm hated the way her pulse beat faster than it should at the side of her neck. Still scared, but out here there wasn't a hell of a lot he could do to make her feel better. Maybe later she'd be up for a damn buddy hug?

"Let's get everyone inside." Sam said. "Jenna. Your bags are in room three-twelve next to the boys."

Puzzled. Jenna's head cocked to one side. "Thanks. But Storm? Where is he staying?"

"Sorry, the place is fully booked. I figured you wouldn't mind sharing rather than drive back to Manhattan tonight."

Well, that sucked. The look of disappointment on her face. He ran the tips of his fingers in a circle over her upper back. "Don't worry about me. Go on with Sam and get settled. I'll deal with the cops."

"Okay. Thanks. See you soon."

He nodded. Glad she hadn't closed the door in his face, he waited for them to go inside. *Still time, bud.* Leaving them for a single second killed him, but the quicker he took care of the local cops, the quicker he could contact Hawke, and get to work on finding out what the hell just happened.

"Go ahead. I'll wait with Jenna and the boys until you're finished." Sam said.

"Thanks. For being here. Letting me know Doc needed help."

"No problem. Now get going, me and George are hanging out for room service. Aren't we boy?"

The seasoned K9 growled low in his throat. He could smell a steak from ten miles.

"I'll wrap things up as quickly as I can," he promised.

"No rush. I'll head to the city once you're done."

"Not staying?" He didn't like the idea of Sam driving in the dark in these conditions, and he was damn sure Snake would be none too happy, either.

"Need to get back before morning. I'm expecting pups."

***

Storm rounded the front of the lodge, still chuckling. Sam and her dogs. He couldn't wait until she and Snake added kids into the mix, sharing their upstate menagerie.

As he approached the flashing lights, three deputies crawled out of the two cop cars pulled up at the side of the road. The senior officer ran his fingers through the few strands of hair left under his cap. his hat.

"Officer Jim Callahan. Hear you've had a heck of a day. Want to bring me up to speed on what went on out there, Mr. er...?"

"Storm." He shook the man's hand. "Not much to tell. Me and Doc Fletcher, Tom's mother, were with the others searching for her son and his friend Jake. Standing on a small ridge, I spotted them below us seconds before someone shot at them. On exfil to the resort, the shooter fired a second time," he reported.

Callahan lifted his chin at the two deputies beside him. "Jones, Schumacher, Peterson is waiting at the rescue truck. Take his statement and have a poke around while you're there."

Not sure how much good that will do. The fucker is long gone. Storm harnessed the thought. Didn't want to put Callahan's nose out of joint.

The officer shoved his hands in his pockets. "Can you describe the gunman, Mr. Storm?"

Storm half-expected the officer to produce a notebook and pencil. "No clear view of his face. Five-ten, stocky build, dressed for the weather in snow camo. Lousy fucking shot."

Callahan scrubbed his chin. "Hunters after the crows. Peterson probably mentioned they are a pain in all our asses this time of the year. How most of them get a permit beats the hell out of me."

Storm shook his head. "This was no hunter." Not the kind that killed birds, anyway.

"Oh, yeah, what makes you so sure?"

"Judging by the sound of the shots, he was firing a shotgun, not a pellet gun or firearm you'd use for hunting crows."

"Sounds like you know your firearms, sir." Callahan scratched his chin, then swooped his index finger under his fake fur collar.

"Ex-military. I work for Sentinel. An international security company."

"That's as may be, Mr. Storm." He smirked. "But we won't draw any hasty conclusions until my men return and we've completed our investigation. Look on the bright side. No one got hurt."

Storm cleared his throat, tempted to ask for his definition of harm. Unless, by some fucking miracle, Callahan's deputies found something at the scene, he figured that would be the end of it. Time to ditch this guy and sic Hawke on the shooter.

"Someone will be in touch regarding the fine."

"Fine?" Storm raised an eyebrow. He knew what was coming, but Callahan's uber relaxed reaction to kids getting shot at pissed him off. Hearing the guy huff with frustration at his question satisfied his petty side. *So sue me.*

"Yep. The small matter of the boys straying from the resort's designated trails."

"Ah. No problem. Can't have that, can we? I'll take care of it."

"See that you do, sir. Are you folks staying here at the lodge?"

"Tonight. Heading to Manhattan first thing."

"Ah, back to the big smoke. Leave all your details with the manager. Have a hunch we will speak again."

"Will do." He nodded before pulling out his phone and filling Hawke in as he walked away.

Eager to check in with Jenna, he headed for their room. When Sam opened the door, and she wasn't there, he couldn't hide his disappointment.

"Jenna's next door making sure the boys are okay." Sam opened the bar fridge and handed him a beer.

"Thanks. Again. Really appreciate you and my best bud being here." He scratched George behind his ears. The K9 blinked and rolled on his back. Legs akimbo, he closed his eyes and waited for the good stuff. Storm chuckled and rubbed the dog's belly.

"Of course. Though I can't say it's been a pleasure. George, you big sook, leave the man alone."

George huffed, licked his hand and returned to sitting by Sam's side.

She grinned. "Well, if you're done with the cops, I'm off."

"Yeah. Questions answered, but I'm sure Callahan will be up for round two once he's checked out the scene. Tell Snake I should be at Sentinel by two at the latest tomorrow." Storm sat and took a long pull on his beer. "Buy George a huge bone. On me."

"Make it two and he'll marry you. Later, big guy." With a two-finger salute, Sam zipped up her jacket and left.

Given he hadn't eaten or slept in hours, he decided against the second beer, flipped on the tv and tried not to count the seconds before Jenna returned.

Chapter Fourteen

Jenna quietly closed Tom's door and leaned against the wall, and for the first time in a long time, drew a full breath deep. Aside from a few scrapes and mild dehydration, the boys were unharmed. She kept telling herself. A good night's rest, plenty of water, and physically, they'd be fine. Armed with enough show and tell to last an entire school year.

For her, the vivid image of her son and his friend ducking bullets was forever tattooed on her brain. Their attempts to shrug off the shooting, make her feel better, deserved an Oscar.

Jake wore his invincible cloak with superhero dedication, while Tom gave her the hug of a lifetime and promised to keep her safe. However, when she made the mistake of asking if they wanted the light on or off, it was a resounding yes.

She understood the noise of a car backfiring would make her jump for the rest of her life. Tears trickled down her cheeks. Wrecked, her hands hadn't stopped trembling. The loud voices from people she couldn't see boomed over the buzz of the lights in the corridor.

Jenna raised her hand to knock on Tom's door, screaming at him to hide, except no words came out of her mouth. A faceless man at the end of the corridor pointed his gun at her. *No.* Her knees buckled. The strong arm circling her waist stopped her from hitting the carpet.

"It's me. You're okay. It's me, Storm."

She wanted to believe him as massive hands, strong and gentle at the same time, cradled her against a solid chest, his steely gray eyes scanning her face. The tone of his voice soothed her, even if she couldn't fully understand all his words, until she had her breathing under control. "I'm tired."

"I know, sweetheart. Let's get you to bed."

Vaguely, she heard herself saying she could walk, then her feet left the ground and Storm was carrying her to their room. It didn't take much before her head sank deep against chest, her cheek at rest in his warmth. He lowered her onto the bed, a very large bed, and sat beside her.

"Sleep. I'll check on you later. Make sure you're okay," he said.

"The bed is big enough for an army. Join me." Jenna patted the pillow. "You must be exhausted, too."

"Relax, Jenna. The chair suits fine. How are you feeling?" He stroked the back of her hand, his thumb skirting the inside of her wrist.

"Er... I'm good." *Liar, liar.* She didn't resist as he entwined their fingers. With the power of a magnet, his tenderness drew her in. His long fingers anchored her. "Honestly? I'll feel much better when we're home." Jenna let go of his hand and peered past him into the bathroom. "Huge shower."

Solid proof she was anything but fine, Storm frowned at her sudden shift in topic.

"Gigantic shower, big enough to..." He nodded slowly.

His eyes were the color of smoke rising from a raging fire. "Shh." With the tip of her finger, she brushed his lips. From now on, thanks to her friends without benefits request, this is what it would be like between them. Off the chart chemistry with no still point.

Storm floated his palm toward the bathroom. "All yours."

A smile tugged at the corner of her mouth. Keeping her distance, a workout, a challenge for every breath. Ignoring their obvious attraction, insisting it was for the best, was dishonest to him and herself.

Since their first passionate kiss, she had wanted to explore this man, body and soul. Risky, letting her guard fall, but loving and losing Rob had taught her nothing was forever. Perhaps she should give Storm a chance.

"Hey. You okay?" Storm pointed at her fist, clutching the crumpled sheet.

Close to cracking, she rested her chin on his shoulder. "I'm sorry."

"For what, sweetheart?"

One by one, Storm uncurled her fingers from the crumpled cotton. Responding with an honest answer was impossible, so she settled for, "putting you and Sam at risk. You could have been ki..."

"Stop." He tapped the end of her nose with the tip of his finger. "I never want to hear you apologize. Not to me. No one got hurt. The boys, you, me, Sam, George, we're safe." He cupped her cheeks in his palms. "None of this is your fault."

Okay, he may be right, but the voice banging on in her brain said, what if danger had followed them from London? Yes, Baxter was dead. She saw his body. But did he have a maniac relative bent on revenge? *Hell, Jenna.* She sounded like one of those characters in the action movies the boys loved.

Storm nudged her arm. "Sleep."

"Impossible. Not tonight. Brain's not ready to let go of what happened. Christ, why would anyone shoot at Tom and Jake?" Tears clogged the back of her throat.

"The cops agree with the dumb hunter theory," he said, a shadow sweeping across his gaze.

"And you? What do you believe?" She sniffed.

Storm shrugged and handed her a tissue from the box on the bedside table. "No harm in considering all options?"

"But? Come on, Storm, talk to me."

"Callahan's take on the situation doesn't sit right with me, either. Hawke's doing some digging, and I told Snake for the next few days I'm not letting you or Tom out of my sight.

A sensible option, one she understood, but deep down the idea of having Storm in her space twenty-four-seven messed with her head. She hated the fact that her ordinary day, the one she and Sam moaned about over a wine and pedicure, lay in shreds.

"You're right, I should sleep," Jenna agreed, because until she figured out how to tell him she didn't think his idea would work, oblivion was best. "But you take the bed. Give those long legs a stretch." He tensed as she tapped his thigh. "I'm going to check on the boys." She could read a book sitting next to their beds. Jenna placed her palms on the mattress and pushed. Unfortunately, her backside refused to shift.

In a single graceful move, Storm helped her to sit on the edge of the bed and sank on his knees in front of her. His gaze traveled from her face to her navel. "Storm." She couldn't make it past his name.

Leaning closer, he tugged on her coat zipper. "You're shivering. Before you go, take off these wet clothes."

"You're right. Should have done it earlier." A simple statement. A fact. Did she have to sound so breathy?

Cool air skittered over her breasts and her nipples pebbled as he took his time lowering the zipper. "St…" Storm, or stop? Before she committed, his finger hooked her chin and tilted her head. Eyes level with his, her insides clenched.

"I think you've got my name handled, sweetheart. Anything else?"

"Yes. No." The tip of her tongue swept across her top lip as she swore the man had a mind to strip her bare, not cup her head, and stroke the edge of his thumb over the pulse fluttering on the side of her neck.

She gasped and told herself to shut the hell up and relax. Allow the universe to handle everything. The tip of his tongue skimmed her blazing skin and traced a slow line along her jaw to her earlobe. Then he sucked, and she saw stars. Bright, twinkling, fairy tale beacons. Christ, the man had moves.

His fingers kneaded and squeezed her breast until her eyes crossed. *Willpower, where the hell are you?* Simple. Carried on her breath, it floated to the ceiling. Jenna shifted, opened her legs, and allowed him to edge closer. His rock-hard erection pressed against her pelvis. A familiar tingle shot from her sex to the base of her spine.

Help. She'd made a deal with herself not to do this, not to get involved. On her next shaky exhale, she dragged herself to her senses. "I'm sorry. Please. Stop."

"Sure." He leaned back.

Scrubbing a hand through his hair, a blank look replaced his smile as cool air rushed into the gap between them. Temper short, she loathed this crushing uncertainty rushing through her blood. She was a doctor, responsible for her actions. Used to taking charge. Crystal clear with her words and intention.

Locked on, she couldn't pull herself away from his gaze. *Own it, Jenna. He's angry. You're a tease.* She'd practically invited him to shower with her. Not because she enjoyed tormenting him. A huge part of her wanted him to whisk her to the intimate places she missed. "I'm sorry," she repeated.

"What did I say, Doc? No need to apologize. It's been a hell of a day. Stay here. Shower and sleep. I'll look in on Tom and Jake, then crash there."

Storm lifted his chin at the armchair underneath the curtained window and winked. "We can take turns if it makes you feel better."

Chapter Fifteen

The wind moaned in the corridor, carrying with it the smell of cooking from the resort restaurant. Storm's stomach growled, Jenna might not be hungry, but he could eat a fucking bear. He pulled the hood of his parka up and over his head and sank into the chair between Jenna and Tom's room.

Arms folded, chin tucked into his chest, he tortured himself, imagined Jenna taking that shower, steamy hot water soothing her naked body, the crook of her finger inviting him to join her. Scrub her back. Wash her hair.

Spin her front to the wall, pin her wrists above her head, nip the pale skin across the top of her shoulders and nudge his cock against the crack between her butt cheeks. Oh yeah, he was all in. A distraction from the distraction was needed before he popped like a teenager in his boxers.

He stretched his legs, fought to pull his cell from his pants pocket, and messaged Hawke.

Storm: Found anything?

Hawke: I'm fast lover, but not Superwoman.

Storm: Not what I heard. Text me as soon as you have something.

Hawke: For the thousandth time. Will do.

Storm rose from his chair, slid the phone into his jacket pocket and counted each dull thud of his boots as he paced in a circle and whistled. Gradually, his libido calmed down and Jenna gradually faded into the background until the dude, needing more than a towel to cover his paunch, stuck his head out of room three-twenty-eight, and demanded he shut the hell up.

The door slammed and flew open again. Storm shrugged in sympathy. Trigger's Rocky ringtone riled most people. "Yeah. What you want?" he snapped.

"Aw. Now is that any way to greet your best friend?"

"Says who?"

"Your mother."

Storm grunted. These days, your mother was his answer to anything and everything. Been watching too many eighties cop shows. "You've added talking to the dead to your superpowers. Impressive."

"Better believe it. Over achiever, that's me. Heard what happened, man. Jenna? The kids?" How they doing?

"Sleeping."

"I take it you're on watch. Call room service. Order some damn ribs or a burger."

"Not hungry," he lied. Didn't want to be caught licking his fingers if hell broke loose. It seldom issued a warning. "Thanks for checking in, dad. You'll be at the meeting tomorrow?"

"Roger that. Sam sent the invite. Whatever you need, man.

That he never doubted. Good to hear all the same. All his Sentinel brothers were there for him, and he for them. Anywhere, anytime. "Catch ya then."

"'Night, Junior."

"Fuck off!" Storm flung his ass into the chair. Amazed it didn't collapse under his weight, he shifted his weary bones and tried to get comfortable. His ass was healing okay but itched like hell.

He could grab his book from his pack. A few chapters of Oliver Twist ought to settle his nerves. Dickens was a mite long-winded for his taste, but he was on a challenge from Winter to read all fifteen of the author's novels.

Only a few hours before sunup, and he could use the bathroom. Without making a sound, or so he thought, he slipped into Jenna's room.

"No need to creep around. I'm awake." Her sleepy voice drifted toward him. "Come here, I need you." Jenna patted the bed cover.

Storm froze. An invitation? A green light? A precious moment when Jenna showed her vulnerability. Should he kick off his boots? Nope keep them on, much less chance of having his pants follow. Perching one knee on the bed, he gathered the woman, fast becoming his everything, into his arms and rolled onto his back. Her head melted onto his chest. Eyes closed, she was half asleep, so he didn't give the gesture too much weight other than her needing a change of pillow.

"Do you think this maniac is here at the resort? No. Forget, I asked. It must be a random shooter. Right? No one would want to hurt the boys. Oh, God, what if he's targeting the resort? An angry-at-the world suicide nut job who takes as many people out as he can before shooting himself," she rambled.

Jenna lifted her head. Tiny puffs of her breath hit under his chin. "Shh. Easy. We will find him, Jenna. I swear. Tomorrow, you and Tom will stay at mine. We can drop off Jake, then go pick up what you need. Snake is arranging for someone to watch Jake and his family."

"What? No. Why?"

"No brainer, Doc. Until we find this asshole, you and Tom are not safe." Storm tucked a stray strand of hair behind her ear. She was so damn pretty, even when her hazel eyes flashed with anger.

But Doc wasn't stupid. She'd see reason. Right? She licked her bottom lip. The way her mouth glistened in the glow from the resort lamps made him horny. Amazing, considering the goddam cold. His balls should be the size of a Mento.

Jen's gentle curves pressed against him, stirring his arousal. He angled his head to the side and kissed her top lip. Waited for her to pull away.

"What are you doing?" she breathed.

"This." He ran the tip of his tongue along the crease between her lips, begging her to open for him.

Her palms pressed against his chest, a tentative push, before she fisted his shirt. But he could see the fear in her eyes. *Don't run.* Desperate to have Jenna choose him over the demons playing in her head, he plundered her mouth with his tongue.

What the almighty hell? He was on watch. Top priority, their safety.

Even if it meant drowning in cold showers. Heart pounding, he swept his tongue over her plush bottom lip one last time and rose from the bed.

"Why did you stop?"

Jenna propped herself on her elbows and stared at him. Hair mussed, eyes bright. *Beautiful.*

"Believe me. I don't want to, but you need sleep and I'm going to take my butt back outside. Just in case there's a lost crow hunter wandering around the corridors."

"That makes no sense. You're exhausted. Could nod off there." She tilted her chin at the chair by the window. "No. Get comfortable. This bed is more than big enough for two." Jenna smiled. "What am I saying? With your super hearing, you'll hear a cockroach sneeze. As I said before. I'm too wired to sleep. I'll keep watch. Wake you if I so much as hear a mouse squeak."

"Jenna. If I climb back on that bed, there is no way I can keep my hands off you."

"And..."

He huffed out a strained laugh. He liked this Jenna, the sexy woman finding the courage to act on what she wanted, as much as he loved the shy, gentle medic. "Distraction, tempting as it is, could prove lethal."

Vulnerable, unsure, her gaze dived to the floor. She shouldn't doubt him. On both counts. Keeping them safe and craving more than a damn kiss.

Without speaking, his brain confused by how much Jenna and Tom meant to him in such a short time, he returned to the chair in the hall.

Around six a.m., the unmistakable sound of a Duck, Hawke's Ducati Multistrada, roared over the incessant purr of the resort's heating system. The squeak of her bikie leathers arrived seconds before she appeared.

"Morning. You been out here all night?" she asked.

"Yep." Staying awake on missions was more usual than not, and his shit attitude had nothing to do with the petite blonde softly snoring behind the door opposite. For the past hour, he'd had listened to her. Kind of comforting in a creepy, domestic bliss, way. "Why are you here? You found something?"

Hawke pushed the tips of her fingers inside the waistband of her pants.

"Kind of, I've checked the situation from all the usual angles plus a few, and you're not going to like it. Fact is, the cops may be right. An idiot with shitty aim. Score one for the crows, zero for Tom and Jake. My guess, the incident will be written up as an accident." She added air quotes around her last word.

"Nah. Doesn't account for chasing our asses. My gut tells me there's more to this, and that piece of gristle is never wrong," Storm groaned.

"Maybe he just got shit scared when he saw you the second time and popped a few in the air. You want me to keep digging?" Hawke threw the question over her shoulder as she headed for the exit.

"You bet. Wait up." He nodded at Jenna's door. "You mind hangin' for ten so I can grab a shower?"

"Sure. Take fifteen. I'm in no hurry."

Hawke settled into his chair and dragged her electronic device from the saddle bag slung over her shoulder. He'd swear she'd been born with the damn thing umbilically attached.

"While I'm here. When you're done, I want to chat with your girl. She may have seen something you missed."

"Not my girl but knock yourself out. Just take it easy. She'd need CPR before she asked for help, but the past forty-eight hours have—"

"Yeah, yeah, tiger. Twinkle Toes is my middle name." Hawke's wink almost took out the side of her face.

"Yeah, right," he grumbled.

Chapter Sixteen

H is back to her, obviously thinking she was asleep. Storm dropped his towel. *Crispy Crumpets.* Jenna sighed. Her libido soared at the sight of his naked butt. Hands down, the rear view was as sexy as the front.

Phone tucked under his chin, his glutes clenched as he balanced on his right leg and slipped his left inside his black cargo pants. Let's hear it for Commando! How she managed not to scream, stop, when his long fingers pulled on the zipper and fastened the button, was a miracle.

She itched to lick his inner thigh from his knee to his ... She groaned. Thanks to her rules, even if Storm allowed it, her dirty thoughts could never leave her head.

As if he sensed her perving on him, he tossed the phone on the chair and turned. A twitch of his eyebrow, her only warning. Quick as a wolf on the hunt, he jumped on the bed and hovered above her. The weight of his long, warm torso covering her, pressing her into the mattress, felt amazing. Solid. Comforting.

His gaze caressed her mouth, the flecks in his gray eyes dancing with amusement. "Like what you see, gorgeous."

"Maybe. And you're nuts. I most certainly am not gorgeous." Jenna giggled. Big clue, her mussed hair and morning breath. Storm smelled as good as he looked. Clean and sharp, the citrus scent of his shampoo hit first, then sank into the smell of an English forest on a rainy day. *Home.*

The clinic at Sentinel wreaked of antiseptic, not always associated with great memories. She turned her head toward the thunder and the rain assaulting the bedroom window.

What would it be like to make love with this powerful man tenderly stroking her skin? Despite her bed hair.

"Mmm," he hummed.

His lips against her throat tickled and sent a shudder rippling down her spine. "What about the boys? Are they awake?"

"Yep. And they've had breakfast. Time to rise and shine, Sleeping Beauty. We're on the road in thirty, and Hawke wants to talk to you before we leave. You, hungry?"

Her pelvis squirmed against the length of his erection. "Yes," she breathed. God, she wanted this man. Their eyes met. *Say goodbye to rules and regs?* Storm hesitated before kissing her forehead and rolling from the bed.

Jenna buried her face in the pillow, afraid if she didn't, she might ask him to stay and finish what they had started. A look, a stroke, that turned her insides to liquid fire. "What does Hawke want with me?"

"Check if you noticed anything I missed. She'll explain."

She almost cried when he slipped the black T-shirt over his head. Damn the man for looking as good clothed as he did without a stitch.

"I'll go chase you up some breakfast. Come on. Get up. Before I toss you over my shoulder and toss you under a cold shower."

"You wouldn't." Jenna held on tight to the sheet. Storm's chuckle rang with clear warning. "Okay, If I must, I must."

"Wise decision, Doc. Brains and beauty." He smiled.

And left. For the best, considering how she struggled with her ridiculous, let's be friends, rule. Still, she had learned the hard way with Baxter.

Like all Sentinel men, Storm was committed to his job. Their women were a special breed, who had no problem when their partners left on a mission. For days, weeks, never knowing when they'd return home.

If she ever considered a relationship, she wanted more than a good lay. And she had no doubt Storm could deliver on that front. Family, surrounded by the cliché white picket fence, more her dream.

****

Showered and dressed, Hawke arrived just as she threw her wash gear and dirty clothes into her bag and zippered it closed. "Come in. Storm said you had questions. How can I help?" Jenna nodded at the chair while she perched on the edge of the bed.

"Thanks. I'll stand. Don't want to hold you up. It's a long drive back, and you guys went through some scary shit yesterday. How are you?" Hawke asked.

Jenna chuckled at the tattooed multi-tasker standing by the door, one eye on her, the other on her phone screen as she flicked through messages. Her stomach rumbled at the sight of the slice of toast slathered in peanut butter in Hawke's other hand. Tall and thin, with spiky black hair, eyes framed with heavy black kohl and blood-red lips added to her scary vampire look.

In some ways her kick ass vibe reminded her of Sam. But no way did she plan on talking to her about the fear making a meal of her gut. People worked hard to get off her stranger list. "How do you and Storm know each other?" she asked while pulling on her boots.

"Answer a question with a question. That's some defensive shield you got going there, Doc. We met in Afghanistan. I was the big guy's civilian liaison. We were both good with our hands." Hawke wiggled her fingers. "I had the tech side covered and Storm the wet work." She slid her index finger across her throat and grinned.

Jenna stopped fiddling with her laces and frowned.

"Ah. Big guy hasn't told you. He's a hand-to-hand combat specialist. If you ask me, those cold steel eyes give it away. The way his team tell it. Their brother knows a thousand ways to kill without pulling a trigger. A touch exaggerated, but he's earned his tag. Storm. A single strike of his lightning-charged mitts and you're dead."

Remembering how he'd held her captive out in the snow, Jenna's breath hitched. His hands were powerful, commanding, but even when he pinned her against the tree, she never feared he'd hurt her. Hard to believe, the fingers gently stroking her tears from her cheek, turning her bones to liquid, were lethal weapons.

His lips? Now that she believed. "Liaison? What sort of things did you take care of for him?" Jenna shoved her arms through the sleeves of her parka. None of her business, even if she ached to know if Hawke and Storm were ever more than work partners?

"We didn't share a room, if that's what you're thinking. I'm not into guys even when they are as hot as the big guy."

"Sorry." Of course. Hawke's bed mate, peering over the sheets on the video text yesterday. She felt her face flush.

"No need. We're close, mainly because I'm a damn wizard at making people appear when they don't want to be found." Hawke reached for Jenna's scarf hanging off the end of the bed and handed it to her. "Helps that I speak eight languages at the last count."

"I'm impressed. You never joined the military?"

"Nah. Me and uniforms are not a good match."

Jenna returned Hawke's smile. The woman was growing on her.

"You? How'd you end up involved with the Sentinel crew?" Hawke asked.

"They needed a medic. I, we were looking for a change."

"We?"

"Now who's fishing? There's just me and Tom."

Hawke grinned. "Kids will be kids, ay?"

"No. If anything, he is the responsible one." Jenna cleared her throat and swung the conversation away from the deep and meaningful of why they'd left London. "Jake, his friend, can be a bit of a muppet." Her laugh sounded false, but she swallowed her next breath and kept talking. "Typical mum. My kid's not the problem. Tom said a guest here at the resort gave them the wrong directions. I believe him."

"Fair. It's a mom thing. But like I told Storm, at this stage, I'm inclined to agree with the cops. An idiot shooter after a crow. Unless you can think of anything, anyone who may want to see you and your son dead?"

Hawke's words hit a nerve. Jenna moved off the bed and tucked the last of her stuff into the side pockets of her bag. "No. Of course not." Hawke shrugged. "Wrong place at the wrong time, except ..."

"Your gut rumbles along with Storm's, telling you two and two, add up to four, plus. When you hit Manhattan, have Storm drive you to E.R. Get your talking insides checked out."

Jenna huffed and grabbed her hat and gloves off the table.

"It's not over until that big girl sings. Isn't that how it goes?" Hawke looped her arm through hers.

Jenna sighed. "Something like that."

"Well, I promised Storm I'd keep digging." Hawke's gaze narrowed. "Have you ever been to Storm's place?"

Jenna frowned at her sudden switch of topic. "No. Why do you ask?"

"No reason. I assumed you'd be staying with him. After what happened, I can't imagine Storm the Protector letting you two go home alone."

"He did offer, but..."

"But nothing. Do it." Hawke nudged her hip.

"Do what?" Storm asked.

Jenna jumped. She hadn't heard him enter. His hand scooped around her waist. "You okay?"

She nodded and slipped from his hold.

"Just suggesting your girl here do the smart thing and stay with you. if only for the view."

"What view?" Even in Brooklyn, few places looked out on anything worth the five-star review Hawke was pushing.

"Thought you were leaving," Storm grumbled, taking hold of Hawke's elbow and easing her to the door.

Chapter Seventeen

Coffee. Storm closed his laptop and headed downstairs to the kitchen. He'd been up since six, thanks to his brain's refusal to shake the incident at the snow. Interrupted sleep wasn't the problem, getting little to no shuteye more normal than not, especially when they were on a mission.

The fact Hawke hadn't been able to shed any light on what really happened in Vermont should have put him square in the middle of a bad mood. Instead, Jenna and Tom, living in his home these past forty-eight hours, left a permanent grin tugging at the side of his mouth.

He hadn't missed the not-so-subtle hints she dropped. How they didn't want to be any trouble, and they should go home. This morning he'd convince her once and for all, staying here with him was the safest place for them until they were sure any threat had been annihilated.

At the sound of her laughter floating up the stairs, his feet picked up pace. Jenna and Tom sat at opposite ends of the kitchen island.

"No." Jenna thumped her fist on the counter.

"Yes." Tom yelled, smiling and frowning at the same time.

"And what's this?" Storm asked, picking a stray Fruit Loop from Jenna's sweater. Her left nipple pebbled under the flick of his finger. So fucking responsive. Brown eyes the color of that coffee with cream he craved stared up at him.

"Tom wants to…"

The kid squinted at her. *Oh yeah.* Doc was a breath away from annihilation if she squealed. She grinned, stretched her body across the granite surface, and tussled her son's hair.

"Hey, it took ages to fix that." Tom pouted.

Every inch the offended teenager, excess gel shone on his forehead. "Looks mad, bro." Storm raised his hand for the kid's high five and felt a hundred years old. Did they even do that shit anymore?

"Okay. I know when I'm outnumbered." Jenna tilted her head. "I made coffee. You want some?"

"You bet." He liked that she read his mind. Her slender legs swung to the sides, and her tiny feet touched the floor. Watching her repeat the move every day for the rest of his life had a lot going for it. Hands up, palms out, because he didn't trust himself not to kiss her, he slipped past her. "Sit, eat your breakfast. I got it. Top up?" He flipped his chin at her empty mug as a piece of cereal shot past his ear.

"No, thanks."

Jenna's long, blond hair swished across his fingers. He squeezed her shoulder, not liking the dark smudges under her pretty eyes. At least two out of three people living in his house hadn't slept last night. Bewitched by her perfect mouth, he leaned in, ready to kiss and claim, but he didn't want to put the kid off his cereal or make her skittish before their big conversation.

Shifting to the bench to pour himself coffee. He held up the pot, offering Jenna a second chance for a refill just as Tom tossed another Fruit Loop at her. It caught the side of her eye and she winced. "Hey, how about you aim for your mouth, bud?" Storm growled over the roaring in his ears. "Not cool."

The kids' eyes narrowed. A glimmer of fear flashed across them before his gaze jack-knifed to his mom. *Goddamit.* Sure, he was mad at the kid for throwing stuff at his mom, but he'd never harm either of them.

"It's okay, love." Jenna squeezed her son's arm. "We were having a discussion. Tom wants to go to school. Has a date with…"

The kid's cheeks turned flamingo red.

"To catch up with a friend," Jenna corrected, sucking in a breath. "Call me over-protective. But I'm not convinced it's such a good idea."

"Tell her, Storm. Even if the guy with the gun isn't a hunter, but a psycho targeting lost kids, how likely is it he's dumb enough to follow us to Manhattan? Zero, right? It's not like he has our address."

Way too many holes in that argument. Caught in the middle, between Doc and her son, he realized how his dad felt when he got a fat no from his mom and begged his old man for his veto.

It blew his mind how he didn't hate wearing the parent hat. But, as much as he wanted more with Jenna, the nature of his work at Sentinel meant he spent days, often weeks, out of country. Not knowing when, or if, he would return wasn't great for family life.

"Well?" Tom urged.

Beside him, Jenna's smile did a shit job of reaching her eyes. Storm sighed. "In my book, a mom's word is law. If she agrees, I can arrange for one of the Sentinel team to take you to school, to your, er, catch up after, then bring you home."

"Cool." Tom threw his arm around Jenna's neck. "Pleeeze."

"I'm not sure. We've caused everyone enough trouble."

"No trouble. Give me two secs to call Snake." He pulled out his phone.

Jenna nodded as she brushed the stray cereal from the table into her hand.

"Thanks, mum," Tom gave her a hug.

"Done. And..." He cornered the boy with a look. "No more Fruit Loop missiles."

"Yes, sir."

Jenna fluttered her hand in front of her pale face. The tear glistening in the corner of her eye gutted him. Tom stood and tucked her in for another hug. "Don't worry, mum. We'll be fine."

"I know. The sooner I get used to you being out of my sight for more than ten minutes, the better. After all, we're going home soon."

The words dropped like lead in Storm's belly. The kid was halfway out the door before he remembered to kiss his mom goodbye. Jenna stared at the empty doorway, hurt walking over her face and fluttering across her chest. "Come here." He pulled her into his arms. "Let's get some air." Taking her hand, he led her out to his small backyard.

Jenna gazed at the cloudy sky. Drops of rain blended with the tears cascading over her cheekbones. "Hey. He's safe with Dexter." The guy was new to Sentinel, but Snake vetted everyone personally.

She swiped her face with her sleeve and sniffed. "My boy is growing up much too fast. I'm not sure I can keep up."

"I take it he has a date with Tina?" Storm winked.

"You know about her?"

"Yeah, her name has come up a couple of times when we've been at the gym. He's smitten." Storm took Jenna's elbow and led her through the broken flowerpots scattered on the ground.

One day soon, he'd get a garden happening. He should leave her alone, give her some space, but his feet had forgotten how to take a direct order, so he tipped his chin at the small iron bench, sat, and thanked the fucking universe when she joined him.

Aware, if he asked her right now to stay, she'd be more determined to leave, he kept his mouth shut. Above the rustling trees, he heard her breath catch. Watching her fight to stop her tears tore him apart.

Storm sniffed in a breath, curled his fingers around Jenna's hand and settled it on his thigh.

"Damn rain." Her next tear landed on their joined hands. "Gets in everywhere," he joked, hoping to make her smile, because sad Jenna played havoc with his mental health.

A nano-second grin flashed his way and spun his world in the right direction. Her slim body nestled against his side, and he wondered how long she could tolerate the closeness. *Who cares? Her pace. Her choice.*

Waiting for her to lift the friends-only bar threatened to fucking finish him. One thing his gut knew, he would spend a lifetime convincing Jenna how much she meant to him.

Rain hammered the tin roof over his back door, bounced off the gutters, and settled in large puddles at the bottom of the steps. Jenna shivered. "You're cold," he grumbled. "We should go inside. Coffee's hot."

"Not yet. I love the rain."

He chuckled. "That's my favorite Brit. Loving the wet and cold is something we will never have in common. Give me the sun and heat any day."

Her nose crinkled. "You sound like Knight."

Founder of Sentinel Security and head of the London op, the Brit loathed rain.

"This is perfect beach weather. Fire Island, here I come. I love Manhattan when it snows." The words caught in Jenna's throat. "Why don't you ask Knight to let you set up an office in California or Texas?"

"You trying to get rid of me?" Storm asked and watched her blush.

"Maybe." Her nose wrinkled.

He loved this side of Jenna, the confident doc. She didn't come out to play often. When she chuckled, her shirt rustled under her sweater. Storm tightened his hold on her hand and buried his chin in the silky hair on top of her head. "I meant what I said. Dexter won't let anything happened to Tom."

"I know."

"So why the tears?"

Jenna stared at their intertwined fingers and sighed. "I was thinking of Rob."

"I see," he muttered and released her hand. *And what kind of twisted jerk envies a dead man?* Hurt and surprise played with the light in her eyes. *Hell.*

"Leaving so soon. Too hot for you?" she asked as he sprung to his feet.

He was making a monumental cock up of this. "No, I'm fine." He sat back down. "You want to talk about it?"

She nodded. "Please."

"Okay. Let's move over there where there's more shelter." With one hand settled in the curve of her spine, he guided her to the rocker under the cover of his token porch. Sam had insisted he buy the creaky chair from a flea market in Westchester. Promised it might come in handy.

Storm sat and patted his knees. The only seat available. Without hesitation, she perched on the edge of his lap, which in his book had to be a positive sign. Wrapping his arms around her, he shuffled her closer.

"It's Rob's birthday."

Seconds felt like hours before he got it together to speak. "Do you have a photo?" *Well done, bud. Flash me the happy snaps.*

Her fingers twitched against his skin. "Yes, I have a few on my phone, but..."

"Show me." *Check out the competition? Fuck me.* Could this get any worse?

Chapter Eighteen

The second Dexter took the bait and rushed to help Jake, Tom sprinted across the baseball pitch. His friend had done him a solid, faking a spectacular head-over-the handlebars fall.

Ducking behind the bike shed, he blew his hair out of his eyes. Despite being forty degrees outside, under the collar of his school shirt, his neck itched from sweat.

He liked Dex, and to be fair, this past week, he had shown a spooky talent for blending into walls, giving Tom space. Today, though, he and Tina needed alone time to discuss serious stuff. Eyes chock full of smiles, she set his blood on fire.

Times like this, he missed his dad. Mum tried, but it didn't feel right talking girl stuff with her. She had her own relationship problems. A couple of months ago, he bet Jake, Storm, and she were going to hook up, but something happened, and stuff got weird.

Shame, because he could tell Mum liked him. In that same shiver, sweat way he felt around Tina. He sighed. Didn't matter how old you got, life loved messing with your head.

Pity Jake didn't like Tina, said she was pushy, acted like the boss of everyone. Laugh out loud. Jake needed to take a long look in the mirror.

He pulled his and Tina's bikes from the racks inside the shed seconds before she rounded the corner on one leg and skidded to a stop in front of him.

"I would kill for mac and cheese," she blurted between pants.

Arms wrapped around her waist, she lifted her head and looked up at the sky as if she expected a plate of her favorite snack to drop out of the clouds. "Okay, let's go to The Hut. My treat," he offered.

"Awesome. But we split the check." Her smile almost completed its journey. "I'll call Mom. Thanks to the detention." She rolled her eyes. "I'm already an hour late, but I don't care. I would do it again. Wendy is a pain in my ass. I deserve a medal for keeping my mouth shut as long as I did. Why this? Why that?" Tina groaned and shuddered the bike handlebars until the bell tinkled. "Who knew a gal had that many dumb questions in her?"

Her wide-eyed jaw drop begged him to agree, so he gave her the chin lift of solidarity, and she rewarded him with one of those smiles. Like the beauty beaming at him right now.

"But when she asked Archer to go over dividing decimals. FFS. The man has droned on for weeks, explaining where to stick the decimal point." She slumped onto the handlebars. "It broke me, Tom."

"Yeah, saw that, but why did you kick her chair?"

"I thought she'd be stunned into shutting the hell up. Didn't expect her to go all Chucky on me and slap my face. Plain bad luck Archer turned as I landed my return smacker." Tina raised her palm.

"Yep. High five," Tom muttered, giving her hand a weak slap. Wendy enjoyed pushing her buttons.

"Hey. I told you not to wait for me," she snapped.

"And I told you, I didn't plan on leaving." He winked and swung his leg over his bike.

Tina didn't have a dad either, maybe that's why he found her easy to talk to. Every day, after school for the last six months, he had ridden with her uptown to her house. Dexter had offered them a lift, but they refused.

"Tell me. All those questions. Is Wendy that clueless?" Tina's brown eyes opened wide.

Tom laughed. "Nah. I reckon she has a crush on Archer."

"Get out of here!" Tina punched his arm. "No way. He must be a hundred years old."

Her laughter trailed after her as she hitched her backside onto the seat, pushed on her pedals, and took off up Park Avenue. Tom gave chase, admiring her thick, black hair, flying at odd angles, tossed by the wind in every direction. Like one of those Valkyries, their English teacher raved about.

At a hundred and fourth street, they leaned into the curve and turned right. Gritting his teeth, Tom shifted gears. Duffy's Hill, the steep climb between blocks to The Hut, killed his thighs. Halfway up, his legs burned, and they were both panting.

Outside her favorite restaurant, Tina pulled to the side of the road and threw her arms into the air as though she'd just completed a Tour de France Mountain stage.

Tom slid in beside her and glanced over his shoulder. The hairs on the back of his neck prickled, same as when he and Jake got lost in the snow. Mum warned him it might take him a while to get over what happened.

"Call the paramedics," Tina groaned and leaned her elbows on her thighs.

"Girl, you are such a drama queen." Tom laughed.

"I'm serious. I'm going to puke." She drew in her chin and retched.

Tom sprang off his bike to avoid the spew, grabbed hers, and rested them against the wall. When she finished heaving, he offered her the napkin he'd saved from his lunch order.

He wanted to kiss her, well maybe not right that second, but at least put his arm around her and give her a hug. Except they hadn't discussed touchy stuff, and he had no clue how to start the conversation.

"You need to get checked out. Remember your appointment at the Women's Hub with mum tomorrow." Before he went to Vermont, Tina mentioned she could be pregnant. "I'm coming with you."

"My hero." She half smiled. "But I think I have something else on."

"Oh no. You promised you wouldn't back out. If you're, you know…" Like a complete jerk, he dabbed his finger at her stomach.

Tina swallowed. "Mom hated me dating Brody. Too young. Concentrate on your schoolwork. Yada, yada, yada. If I am pregnant, she will crack it."

Tom pictured breaking Brody's nose. When Tina first told the creep, she may be having his baby, he refused to take any responsibility and said he'd swear she lied if she called him out as the father. Who does that?

Tina sniffed and wiped her wrist across her mouth. "Jesus, I don't want to hurt my mom."

"I get it. One step at a time. If you want, my mum will talk to her, help her understand."

"Yeah? Well, riddle me this, hero. Why don't you ever touch me?"

Tom's stomach flipped, the way it did when she dropped a question bomb. Shy was never her problem. "Tina, I…" Afraid he'd give a wrong answer, he bit his tongue until he tasted blood.

"Forget it. Do you think your parents had sex before they married?" Tina's grin took the edge off the frosty air.

"I'm sure they did. Math isn't my best subject, but I can add, and the date on their wedding certificate doesn't lie. I arrived way too early." He shrugged.

Tina's jaw dropped.

"Will you keep it?" he mumbled, sure he shouldn't be asking.

"Don't know. And that makes me feel worse because that should be an automatic yes. By the way, it's not an it."

"No, right, sorry. If you do. I'll help." Digging deep he found the courage to reach out and touch her, just as the car roared out of nowhere. Speeding over the crest of the hill, headlight on full beam. Blinding him.

"Shit. Who is this jerk?" Tina yelled and dived in front of him before he moved out of the way.

Her elbow whacked him hard in the chest, knocking him into the chairs crowding the sidewalk. The car hit, and Tina went flying. Her screams kept coming until she hit the road.

"No." Tom yelled as the Prius tore into the gas station opposite. With one hand on the wheel, the driver peered at them through his rear window and revved his engine.

Heart pumping, fear colliding with anger, amazed he hadn't shat his pants, Tom ran to Tina and fell on his knees beside her. Above his head, people screeched.

He didn't take his eyes off Tina. If the guy came at her again, he would have to go through him before he hit her. People ran toward the driver, waving and yelling at him as he swerved out of the gas station. Tires squealing, he turned and slipped into the stream of downtown traffic.

"Tina." Blood pooled beneath her long, dark hair. He grabbed her hand and brought it to his lips. "Everything's okay," he told her, saying the words over and over, because that's what he'd want. To know someone was there for him.

"Someone call an ambulance." He pleaded. Tina saved his life by jumping in front of him. "Why did you do that?" he whispered, willing her heart to keep beating.

Tom stiffened as they lifted Tina onto a gurney and loaded her into the ambulance. Unease slithered down his spine, and he went to climb in beside her, but the paramedic shook his head.

"Sorry, son. No room. She'll be okay," he said, patting him on the head as if he were a good dog.

Bullshit. "She's my friend. Where are you taking her?"

"Columbia. Not far. Meet us there." The paramedic pulled the doors shut.

Tom didn't take his eyes off the ambulance as it left. Sirens blaring.

Chapter Nineteen

J enna let out an enormous sigh of relief and hit send on the last email for the day. *Finally.* She loved her job, but this was one morning she should have pulled the covers over her head and stayed home. Her plans for the day had gone to hell before she finished her first coffee of the day.

To cap it off, as she was leaving the Women's Hub that afternoon, a woman had stumbled into the clinic needing immediate medical attention. Cracked ribs and a concussion. Thanks to her partner's fists.

Her gut twisted tighter than a neurotic pretzel. She wanted to castrate the guy. Triggered and angry, she arrived at Sentinel, unable to concentrate on anything other than routine jobs. Stocking the Bergan Packs ready for the next mission, answering more sodding emails.

With a groan, she slammed her palm onto the wooden desktop and rattled the pen holder. Remembering the reports she had to finish before crawling into bed tonight, she closed her eyes and counted to ten. First. Carbs.

She wasn't a great cook, but she made a mean pesto pasta suffocated with sundried tomatoes and parmesan cheese. What's not to love? Tom and Storm agreed.

Breathe. After food, time to indulge in Storm's porcelain spa bath. He convinced her to stay another couple of days, and she'd miss the luxury when she went home.

Jenna closed her clinic door before the man in question poked his head around it. Given her dark mood, she might bite it clean off. These past few days, he had gone out of his way to make things easy for her and Tom. And, aside from the occasional hand holding, the warmth of his palm on her back when he guided her to the car, he respected her request and hadn't tried to kiss her. Deep down, she wished he had, which proved her point. No willpower.

When her anxiety raged and she demanded answers, Storm remained calm as she ranted. Why hadn't the police, Sentinel, the best damn security business on the continent, found the maniac who shot at Tom and Jake? Did she expect Storm to snap his fingers and conjure the moron? To her shame, yes, she did.

He played peacemaker when she wanted to strangle Tom for being a teenager. Hell, the man held her close, his palm stroking her back, and offered reassurance when she cried over Steve's photo. They ought to bottle his strength and push it through an I.V. line to her clinic patients. There were at least ten who would benefit.

Difficult didn't come close to describing single parenting, and Storm had the patience of a pregnant elephant. Her heart softened whenever she saw him with Tom. They never shared what they talked about during their workouts in his basement gym, but she appreciated her son had someone to talk to other than his over-protective mother. Best of all, the light had returned to her kid's eyes.

Often, she caught a glint in Storm's gaze, the tilt of his head. Unspoken signals. He wanted to kiss her, but one brush of his full, luscious lips, and...

She missed being touched. Longed to be held after a tough day, but that weakness, the loneliness, led to Baxter, the first man who had winked at her. She despised herself for allowing him to manipulate her. Desperation could kill. It almost had.

Lying in bed, before she fell asleep or woke in the morning, she admitted to herself and her pillow how much she trusted the Sentinel warrior to keep her and Tom physically safe. And, she suspected, with her heart. Before things got out of hand, they had to go home and resume normal.

Jenna opened her eyes and glanced at the cute clock on the shelf above her desk. I LOVE. The words arched over the giant red apple in the center. A welcome to New York gift from the man himself.

And there she was, full circle, unable to blast the memory of his scorching kiss into oblivion. Where was Tom? Dexter usually dropped him at Sentinel by five, starving, ready to go back to Storm's and eat.

Jenna swiped the back of her hand over her forehead. Fear trickled through her veins. This crippling insecurity had to stop before she smothered Tom.

He had a major crush on Tina. Wouldn't be long before he started dating for real. Most likely, that's where he was, stealing a few extra minutes with her. Remembering the kind of attraction when leaving someone caused physical pain, tears pricked the corner of her eyes.

Jenna rubbed her upper arms. The heat had switched off early this evening and the early evening chill had found her office. She checked the clock. *Hurry, baby.*

"Time to go home."

She hadn't heard the door open, but she recognized the deep rumble of Storm's voice. He stood in the doorway, the light in the corridor landing on the small scar on his chin.

Her gaze wandered over his rugged shape. The muscled arms folded across his chest. Confidence rolling off him in waves. "Sorry, I didn't realize you were waiting for me. You, go."

"Why would I do that?" he said. One eyebrow arched.

Okay, so he hadn't let her drive alone since the shooting. "No really. Dexter and Tom will be here soon. I'll lock up and catch a lift to yours with him. They're late. He's probably chatting with Tina. I'm trying not to worry. Did you know she's booked an appointment at the Hub tomorrow?"

She knew better than to lay her insecurities at Storm's feet. Now he'd never leave without her.

"I heard," he said.

His gray eyes studied her, and she didn't feel as chilled. Instead, a familiar warmth caressed her shoulders. "You did?"

"Yep. Heard he's working up the courage to ask her to the Prom, too. I gave him my best pointers, shared my wisdom."

"I'm sure you did. Tell me more." *Terrific, Jenna.* Instead of holding the boundary, she gave Storm a boost over the wall.

Three strides and he stood in front of her. His sure fingers stroking a stray curl from her face. "If you're staying, I'll make us a cuppa. How do you like your tea? Milk, sugar?" She reached for her empty cup.

"As you know. I never touch the stuff."

Damn the man for being more adorable when he sulked. "Oh, for heaven's sake. Grow up. If we can't be friends, working together is going to be difficult. Should I be looking for another job?"

"No. I apologize. And don't worry about Tina. Her appointment is a good thing, right?"

"Yes. Of course." Too many young women left it to the last minute before checking birth control options. At least, that's what she assumed she needed. Not wanting to think about sex and her son, she straightened her spine.

"As for us. We can go slow, Jen," he said softly.

Hell. Tempted. And when did he start calling her Jen? She ran her fingers through the short hairs on his temple. Could she be this woman, Jen? "What's your real name?" Ever since her conversation with Hawke, she'd been curious.

"I'll never tell," he whispered in her ear.

"Why? Is it weird? A secret? Please."

"I like it when you beg."

His low laugh rumbled under her hand. She had no idea when it wandered to his chest. "Hilarious, big guy." Her light thump on his pec carried her heavy day with it. "Pretty please. Give it to me."

"Your wish is my command, Princess."

"Your name, idiot. I swear. If you don't stop with this..." She waved at the space between them. "Stuff. I will..." Instead of backing off, Storm feathered kisses over her frown. Her insides clenched. Her pussy burned. *Oh my God.* "Please."

"Please, what?"

Her phone vibrated on the desk. *Saved.* She dodged under his arm. Her body may have escaped, but her eyes refused to leave him. "Jenna speaking."

"Mum?"
"Hi, darling."
"Mum?" he repeated, his voice shaky.
"What's wrong, love? It's late. Where are you?"
"Don't be mad. It's Tina, she's..."
"Where's Dex..." Their words collided.
"I'm at the hospital. He's killed her."

Chapter Twenty

Storm exhaled and tried to rein in his seething anger. Tina, a fifteen-year-old school kid for Christ's sake, mown down in broad daylight. Sure, this was New York City, where shit happened, but this kind of crazy transcended bad luck. The driver who fled the scene had better hope the cops caught up with him before he found the mother fucker.

Jenna glanced over her right shoulder at him, fear trailing behind her as the doors to Emergency swung shut.

"Tina Flores. MVA. Paramedics brought her in recently." She pressed her fists into the counter, separating her from the nurse on duty.

Perched on tiptoe was a different woman than the scared mom who sat beside him on the drive uptown. Doc wanted answers. She raised her eyes to the roof. Praying? Hanging onto the interterrestial kicked logic's ass when chaos blew your world apart.

"And you are?" The nurse frowned.

"Doctor Jenna Fletcher. A friend. Tina Flores. My son, Tom, was with her when the accident happened."

"Oh, I see." The chair groaned as the nurse twisted to get a better look at her screen.

"ASAP," Storm muttered, loud enough for Jenna to hear. The swift elbow jab caught him in the ribs. Her face flushed. Moments before, she had been paler than the sheet covering the gurney pushed against the opposite wall. He half smiled. More than happy to take another blow, if it meant she had found her spark.

"Please, where can we find her?"

At the sound of worry returning to her voice, he almost reached for her hand, and opened his big fat mouth to tell her everything would be okay. Except Doc deserved better than that swipe at her intelligence.

"Please." Jenna's jaw firmed.

"Just a moment, honey." The nurse wiped her nose with a tissue and jiggled her computer mouse.

Jenna twitched at the sudden flutter and raised voices coming from behind the cubicle curtain to their left.

"Shit, no. You ain't gonna touch me with that damn thing. Let me outta here," a man yelled.

Startled, Jenna swung from the desk and faltered. Cupping her elbow, he steadied her. She tugged hard, but didn't get to pull away, not until he confirmed there was no threat to her safety. "It's okay. You're safe," he growled. Eyes glittering with molten heat dipped to where her breasts brushed against his chest.

"You fucking touch me, man, and I'll gut you with this."

Hell no. Several orderlies rushed behind the curtain. Slim chance patients followed through, except, lately, situations turned strange real quick.

He released Jenna's arm and grasped the handle of the push knife, a small, lethal blade secured in the sheath, pressed against his lower spine. The nurse's eyes, sporting a so what's new expression, remained locked on her screen as she tilted her head toward the curtain.

"Pay him no mind, hon. He's a regular. Ain't killed nobody I'm aware of, but I guess there's always a first time." A normal day at the office. She peered at Jenna over the rim of her glasses.

"Tina? Your friend? Says here, they have taken her to Radiology for a CT scan. Take the elevator." Her specs returned to the perch on top of her head.

"Thank you for your help," Jenna said, her voice too shaky.

"You're welcome, hon. Now, let's see what's got him all worked up this visit."

Keeping his body angled between her and the curtain doing floaty shit, Storm guided Jenna to the elevators. As the doors closed, he punched out a text to Dexter. *What the hell had happened?* More to the fucking point. Where was he? From the beginning, Tom had been hell bent on giving the ex-marine the slip. Hard to believe he'd succeeded.

Jenna huddled in the corner of the elevator, shaking her head. "I'm scared, Storm. It doesn't make sense. The shooting, now this."

"I hear you. And I promise. I will find out who did this."

"You said that before," she murmured.

And both times he meant it. Given neither Sentinel nor the cops had found anything on the shooter, his words meant shit. Goddamit, he'd let her down, but it didn't stop him from reaching for her, turning her back to his front, and kneading the ridge of tight muscles across the top of her shoulders.

In silence, they stared at the numbers, crawling floor to floor until they landed at Radiology. The elevator pinged, and Jenna took off. For a breath, his greedy hands hovered in front of him.

Tom sat motionless in the waiting area. As one, they swamped him in a massive hug. "How you going, bud?" The kid shook his head and buried his face deeper into his mom's shoulder.

Ashamed, Storm eased out of their circle. He should never have handed responsibility for Tom's safety to Dex. For damn sure, if he had been watching out for the kid's safety, this might never have happened.

"Wait here with Storm, love, while I check on Tina. I'll be right back, okay?" Jenna said, her gaze fixed on him as she cupped her son's head and kissed his hair.

Storm nodded. "I'm right here, bud." *For as long as it takes.*

***

Jenna's breath shuddered as she made herself do the one thing she didn't want to do. Leave her son. He must remember the last time they waited on uncomfortable chairs, staring at apple green walls, the smell of antiseptic and over-cooked hospital meals wafting over their heads. Her stomach churned with the memory of the day his dad passed.

Nervous energy ran through her veins as she paced outside the CT scan, waiting for someone to give her an update. Had Tom called Tina's mum? Acid bile stung her mouth just thinking of her sitting at home wondering why her daughter wasn't home.

Time moved in slow motion until the pretty blonde, Christ, she didn't look much older than Tom, appeared. Jenna offered her hand. "Hello, I'm Doctor Fletcher, Tom's mum. My son was with her. How is she?" Her gaze flashed to the wall separating them from the girl who held her son's heart.

"Good evening, I'm Doctor Ames, Assistant Radiographer. Doctor Chalmers is with Tina. Are you a relative?" she asked, before hiding her hands in her pockets.

Jenna rubbed her fingers along her pants. Reaching out overstepped the mark. "Er, no. Friend. They were on their way home from school." Her breath hitched. "He's devastated."

"Water?" Doctor Ames pointed to the cooler in the corner.

"Yes. Thank you." Jenna took a paper cup from the holder. Ice-cold liquid punched the back of her throat and rolled like a boulder through her windpipe.

"Doctor Fletcher. As a result of the accident, Tina suffered multiple injuries, and I'm afraid..."

Her heart beat faster as a man appeared, his face ashen. Fumbling for the seat behind her, she sank into it. She'd been in Chalmers' shoes many times. Jenna straightened her spine and braced for the bricks to fall.

Hands stuffed into the dark comfort of his pockets, he rocked on his feet. "Mrs. Flores?"

"No." Her breath faltered. She jumped to her feet. "I'm Doctor Fletcher. A friend. My son is..." All the words, hand wringing, and prayers couldn't stop this. Her eyes closed, then opened wide. *Ready.*

"I'm very sorry, Doctor Fletcher. Tina, Ms. Flores passed away." He glanced at his watch. "Six minutes ago."

Jenna clutched the edges of her coat. Chalmers kept speaking, but his words, clichés, failed to register. How on earth could she face Tom?

"Will you or the police contact Tina's next of kin?"

"I will." Jenna said, fighting a shiver.

"I'm very sorry for your loss, Doctor Fletcher."

"Thank you."

"Staff will take Miss Flores to the morgue. When you speak with her family, tell them they will have to talk to the police."

With their hands still in their pockets, Chalmers and Ames walked away. Jenna sucked in a moment, then grabbed another, before going back to where she'd left Tom and Storm.

"Mum?" Her son jumped from his chair.

Storm placed his palm on Tom's shoulder. He towered over her son. Always there. Ready to catch them when they fell. Her son lurched into her arms. "Darling, I'm so sorry, Tina is... She's gone, sweetheart."

Chapter Twenty-One

Storm would cut off an arm for a chance to turn back the clock on the last couple of hours. Jenna and Tom walked in silence on either side of him into the hospital underground car park. Concrete walls muted the world outside while unsaid voices competed with the chaos inside their hearts and heads.

He enjoyed impossible situations, excelled at figuring his way out of unimaginable shit, but he struggled to find any words. He felt inadequate, inept. Small. Fucking impotent. With no clue how to eradicate the pain of Tina's brutal death. Murder, according to Tom.

"Food." Storm blurted. Not a question or an answer, simply the best he had to offer. Jenna nodded. With a shrug, Tom didn't stop watching his feet as they paced his torment.

"Sounds good. Where?" Jenna asked. The fake brightness in her voice pierced his soul.

"I know a place." He pressed the button on his key fob and the doors opened.

"Tom, you want the front seat, love?" Jenna stroked her son's upper back.

The kid didn't so much as blink as he climbed into the back seat of the car. Tires screeched on the ramp to their left. Jenna flinched. Storm shook his head—just an eager shit with the luxury of believing his life was a race.

For a sec, he sat behind the wheel racking his brain for that quick fix to lighten the mood and waited for everyone to fasten their seat belts. His Sentinel team relied on him to be their comic, to lighten the mood when life got tough.

Twenty agonizing minutes later, he pulled up outside Casa Pete's. With any luck, tonight's jazz vibes might soothe sorrow dangling over their heads.

"Evening, Storm. Haven't seen you around." Pete, one of his old Delta Force buddies, slapped him on the back. The scar etched into the side of his face crinkled with his smile, loaded with a comrade's tenderness. Storm flinched, afraid he'd lose it if he didn't put some space between them.

"Table three."

Pete caught his drift and flicked his chin at a booth in the corner, away from the crowd. Close enough to get lost in the music. "Thanks, bud."

Pete frowned, but when no one elaborated, he didn't push.

"Sit. I'll bring water and menus."

With his hand against Jenna's lower back, Storm led them to the booth. When she sat, Tom shot to the other end of the curved bench, the furthest spot from his mom, and waited for him to take the spot in the middle.

Jen ducked her head and wiped a tear from the corner of her eye. He was all set to ask the kid why he needed to punish his mom when menus toppled in front of them. "Thanks. Full house, tonight."

"Always when Lena's in the kitchen. I swear the patrons smell her food on Staten Island."

"True." Lena's cooking was off the planet good.

"Better keep moving. I'll be back to take your order, pronto." Pete dipped his chin at Tom, a questioning look on his face.

Storm shook his head. "No worries." Reaching for the carafe of water, he poured everyone a glass and opened his menu. "If Lena's on, I suggest nachos, followed by her fried chicken tacos." Jenna turned green. Dumb idea bringing them here.

"No." Tom's barely audible voice sank beneath the clash of plates and the buzz of voices.

"Sorry, sweetheart?"

Jenna reached across the table for her son's hand, but he avoided contact. *Yeah, I get it.* When feelings were close to the surface, skin-on-skin connection killed every time.

"Tom?" Jenna's voice hitched.

"No." Louder, stronger—the kid was gonna bolt. Ready to chase, Storm inhaled through his nose.

"Wait," Jenna called after him as Tom pushed the immovable table and vaulted for the exit sign.

"Stay." Storm caught Jenna's trembling wrist and pecked the top of her head. "I'll go."

He slowed his pace. There was no point crowding him. The kid didn't know the builders had switched the signs during the renovations. A mistake Pete never had fixed. No exit, buddy, just the men's room.

Outside the locked door, listening to Tom sob his heart out, gutted him. He tilted his head to the low ceiling and closed his eyes. Did he knock or take the coward's way out, leave him alone and go back to Jenna?

He knocked. "Tom." Jeez. Enough with single words playing at being a sentence. Palm pressed against the door, he took a deep breath. "Let me in, bud."

"No." Okay. Some habits die hard.

"Please." Storm swallowed. "I need you." *What the almighty fuck.* The truth hit him in the solar plexus and pushed a boulder to the back of his throat.

The door clicked open. A chance. Storm edged the gap wider with the toe of his boot and slipped inside. A chill pulled on the hairs on his forearms. Tom sat on the floor in front of the basin. "Tight spot, my friend." With a groan, Storm arranged his six-three frame in the tight spot beside the kid.

"You getting old?"

A flicker of a grin passed over the kid's pale face. *Smart ass.* But he'd count the three words as success.

"Watch your mouth." He chuckled. "You okay?" The shit people said when they had nothing to say.

"Tina, all this." The hand resting on Tom's knee flipped through the air. "It's like a bad dream I can't, don't want to forget. It doesn't make any sense."

He was still sorting his way through the platitudes when Tom hit him with the big guns.

"What are we living for, Storm?" The kid looked him dead in the eye.

There had to be a million possible answers out there, but he doubted any of them led to the truth worth a fucking bean. His single word reply blew him away. "Love."

Tom cocked his head to one side, confusion swirling in his teary eyes. "I don't get it."

"Me, either. But it's true." He paused. Tom deserved more, so he kept right on blabbing. "For me, in any case. Your mom is breaking up inside for you, Tina. Her head busting with sad stuff, memories. Your old man. Yet love for you beams out of her. It's contagious." He hooked the kid's neck and kissed the top of his head. "See."

Tom rolled his lips together, a single tear rolling down his cheek. "I haven't got around to telling her yet, so let this be our secret, but I love your mom. You, too, if you'll let me, and it scares the bejesus out of me. It's tearing me up, not having the perfect way to make this all go away." Suddenly, looking the kid in the eye was impossible. His chin dropped to his chest. "I'm so damn sorry, man."

"It's not your fault, and I get it. Will you promise me something?" Tom nudged his elbow.

"Anything. Ask."

"When you find whoever did this, swear you will end him with maximum pain."

A kid after his own heart. "Trust me. Bet on it."

Tom held out his hand. A small, steady, strong hand. A hand any man would be proud to shake. "What do you say? Ready to go out and show your mom the answer to the meaning of life."

"Uh, huh. And Storm. Don't hurt my mum."

"Never." They left the restroom, shoulder to shoulder. Damn, it felt right. Now to convince Jenna they had a chance at family. Today's tragedy had dug a deep trench in their lives, and he feared more lurked out there, waiting to make another move.

Storm couldn't resist a snort. The fucker who murdered Tina didn't have a clue what kind of tornado twisted his way.

Chapter Twenty-Two

S hep bit his tongue, sniffed and cursed the pain taking bites out of his right knee. Hand braced against the wall, he tapped his keycard with the other and dragged his sorry ass into his hotel room. It killed to put weight on his leg, so he hopped forward and nudged the door shut with his elbow.

Kids. He'd had a gut full of sharper than a cheese grater minions. Especially the dumb girl who jumped in front of his target. Who did that shit? And why the fuck he swerved was a mystery. The high-speed wrench from accelerator to brake finished his already messed up knee.

Shep lowered his foot and took a step. *Mother fucker*. Tiny black dots swam in every direction. Thank Christ his room was no bigger than a Twinkie and the wall stopped him from falling.

Gingerly, Shep swung his weight to the left, reached through the open bathroom door and snatched a towel from the rail. Pivoting in the narrow space, he grabbed the ice tray from the bar fridge and banged it on the counter hard enough for glasses on the shelf above to rattle. The blocks must have been there for months because the extra crusty bits around the edges of the yellowing plastic didn't budge.

With two fingers, and the help of a spoon, he salvaged a couple of cubes and tossed them into a glass. The rest he rolled in the cheap, thin towel.

What doesn't kill you makes you stronger, his gran loved to say as she beat him with the yard broom. Bourbon by the bottle. Her answer to every one of God's mighty challenges.

Shep tore the tops off most of the miniatures in the minibar, poured himself a large cocktail, and raised his glass to the picture of gran sitting on the bedside table. "Cheers." Long dead, but his lucky charm never always traveled with him on a job. Not so goddam lucky today.

The damp towel stuffed under his armpit, the alcohol clutched in one hand, Shep hopped three times and made it to the side of the single bed. Leg stretched to the max along the thin bedcover, he swung the other over and sank into the thin mattress. Hallelujah, he didn't spill a drop of his medicine.

With a throaty chuckle, he placed the glass on the bedside table. Leaning forward, he smothered his swollen knee with the icy towel. As close to bliss as he'd felt in a hell of a long time. Shep reached for his drink and downed the juice. "Whoa!" That cheap shit had bite. The stuff made his eyes water.

Setting his empty glass down, he took a deep breath and laid flat. The mattress springs dug into his ass. Another, every expense spared, motel comfort. Call this shithole a room and gran's god wouldn't think twice before striking you down. "Ain't that the truth, you ole bitch?"

Shep growled at the nagging pain in his knee. Worse by the second, but a trip to Emergency was too risky. Witnesses to his bungle had their fucking phones trained on him as he fled the scene. By now, his face was all over the internet.

He angled his body at the in-house phone and dialed nine for room service. Hell, he'd tip the person who brought him a keg of bourbon. Green numbers on the bedside radio-clock reminded him Hassan usually called around this time wanting his update. Son-of-a-bitch lived for them.

No way did he have the energy to pull the blinds, so he covered his eyes with his forearm and debriefed his day. Number one. Tom had more lives than an alley cat. Shep pincer gripped his knee. His goddam leg was on fire. Two. Not his damn fault, but kinda shame about the girl. Unlike the boy's whiny ski buddy, she deserved better.

Earlier, playing his favorite, what if, game with her life, he'd pegged her future as a high-class hooker earning more money than Croesus. Her nubile body was built to tease the likes of him. Unfortunately, given her sacrificial nature, she would most likely give most of her earnings away to a stray dog's home.

Pity he wouldn't have the benefit of seeing that one play out. The way her head crunched against his side panel, she was as dead as the postage stamp sized tv hanging on his wall.

Granted, he didn't hang around to make sure, but his gut assured him his instincts were on target. Three. Say so long to any bonus from Hassan after this and his last goat rodeo in the snow.

Shep winked at gran's photo. She loved that one. *Goat rodeo.* He scratched his chin and made a perfect circle with his lips. "Ho, ho, ho." He chuckled.

"Okay, gran. Hasan will go ballistic when he hears I messed up killing the kid a second time, right?" As if he didn't know, but he asked out loud and flicked his gaze to the chair squeezed against the wall by the window.

The phone by the bed shrieked. *Jesus.* Like everything else in this flea pit, it didn't just ring, it rattled. He rolled to his side. Melted ice oozed from the skimpy towel, and a burst of cold water seeped down his thick into the crotch of his jeans. *Fuck! Shit!.*

Shep grabbed the phone. "Yeah. I said as many itsy-bitsy bottles of Bourbon as you have, pronto," he yelled.

"Celebrating, Shep?"

"Huh?" Fear hurled him upright. Fucking Hassan. Crossed wires, or what? "Er, no, boss." He winced and shuffled his weight into a more comfortable position.

"Why not? The boy is dead. Yes?"

The slime ball made ordering a milkshake sound like the end of the world. "No." Shep kept his voice steady, stroked his knee, and did his damndest to make out he had shit covered. The snort in his ear said, try harder.

"What happened?"

"Don't want to bore you with the whole story, boss. His friend, er, got in the way. Pretty sure she's dead, and I'll finish Tom tomorrow. Word is the girl meant a lot to the kid." He threw the latter in as a lame sweetener.

"I need more expense money." Yeah. Like that was going to happen. He'd be out of pocket on this one, and still up to his damn eyeballs in debt.

"Thank you, Shep. That will not be necessary. Your services are terminated."

"Now listen here, dude." In agony, he dragged himself off the bed, lifted the phone from his ear, and hollered into the mouthpiece. "What about my money?" Fucking priorities. Right?

His answer, a faint click. Goddam, son-of-a-bitch. Shep ripped the phone from its socket and hurled it against the wall. The sudden move threw him off balance, and his ass hit the floor. He eyed the empty glass sitting on the bedside table above him.

Shep sucked in a breath, formed his fingers into a gun and named every one of the wavy lines crisscrossing his vision. "Tom." He blew imaginary smoke from the end of the barrel. "Jenna, boom, Hassan, boom, boom." And anyone else who got in the goddam way. This crazy shit was over today. He flung himself back onto the bed. Okay, tomorrow. Once he managed some shut eye.

Chapter Twenty-Three

Back at Storm's, Jenna left Tom's room. Reluctantly, he'd taken the mild sedative she offered him and should sleep through the night. Exhausted, she clung to the banister and finally allowed her tears to fall.

Five minutes later, she had made it almost to the bottom of the stairs before she stopped to watch Storm light the fire in the brownstone's old fireplace.

Showered and changed, his damp, wavy hair licked the neck of the black T-shirt that molded to the contours of his shoulder blades and the nubs of his long spine. Crouched beside the grate, his muscled arse and solid thighs strained against his denim jeans. Again, it crossed her mind that his rear view was sexier than the front. Almost.

The last stair creaked under the weight of her foot. Difficult to creep around the magnificent old building Storm called home. Although he had no trouble. Three of his space efficient strides, and his hands cupped her cheeks.

From under hooded lids, blue-gray eyes searched her face. Storm's intense gaze mirrored her sadness, and she couldn't tear herself away. Never had she felt this close to anyone, including Rob. Yet, in the same heart stopping moment, it felt like a million uncrossable miles separated them.

"You? Tom? You're okay?" His deep baritone voice rumbled beside the thunder.

"He's pretending to be asleep," she gulped.

"Stands to reason. He needs time by himself."

Bullseye. His words struck like a tomahawk. The gremlin eating at her soul screamed, *terrible mother*, and she lashed out. "I'm not stupid." Her voice cracked.

"Jen."

Storm's thumbs stroked the tears from her cheeks. "Sorry. That was mean, it's... Oh, God. I feel so bloody helpless. Murdering a defenseless teenager. Not bothering to stop, leaving her there like a pile of rubbish. If I get my hands on the bastard, I will castrate him and cheerfully watch him bleed out while I stick pins in him. I..."

"Hey, easy." His hand cradled the back of her neck and brought her forehead to his solid chest. "My bad, sweetheart," he murmured against her ear. "I didn't mean to upset you. And, for the record, I'm the only idiot here. Forgive me."

"Nothing to forgive. It's been a crap couple of weeks." Reluctantly, she eased off his chest and squeezed her eyes shut.

"Hey, look at me." His fingers curled around her shoulders. "We will get him, Jen. I swear."

Christ, she envied his confidence. His strength. Her head thumped against his chest. Since they left the hospital, her world hadn't stopped spinning. His friend's restaurant slipped into a blur.

Reluctant to give up the sanctuary of the arms circling her waist, she rested in the refuge of his embrace, and listened to Storm's strong, regular heartbeat pulsing against her cheek.

None of them could move on for real until they caught the SOB who'd shot at them and killed Tina. She may be powerless to do too much on that front, but... "Storm?"

***

"Ask, Jen. Anything." *Say the word and I will lay the cosmos at your feet.* Without sacrificing an inch of body contact, he cupped her face. "What do you need?"

Looking into her beautiful hazel eyes, he slowly exhaled. His lips hovered close to her mouth, craving a kiss from the woman who called him, friend.

Despite what she'd been through, the Neanderthal inside wanted to strip her naked right there in his fucking living room, lay her out on the sofa beside the fire and feast on her until she lost control. Begged him to fuck her. Slow and soft, hard and fast, and any combination in between while he drank in every whimper, savored every shift of her expression as he drove them both to the edge.

"Any chance of a ..." Her voice faded, mid-sentence, as though she hadn't quite figured out what, and expected Tom to appear on the stairs behind her.

"Every chance." He tilted her chin and brought her eyes level with his.

"I haven't asked yet. You may say no."

Not a fucking chance. "Try me."

"Can I use the shower in your room? It's closer to Tom, in case he needs me." The words tumbled from her lips.

"Sure." He brushed a strand of hair behind her ear. "Let me scrub your back."

Their gazes locked. The twist in the middle of his chest tightened. The desire to take her, love her, barked like a rabid dog in his head.

"Please." The tip of her tongue swept between her lips.

His body reacted to the husky tone in her voice, and he pounced. "I have the perfect piece of equipment." The time to explore the attraction burning between them was right here. Right now.

Her eyes flared.

Fuck, no. He tightened his grip on her arms, afraid Doc would follow her flickering eyelids and run. "Loofah gloves."

"Hot damn." Her giggle shredded the gloom of the past hour.

"Jeez. That's two cuss words in less than ten minutes, Doc. Never knew you it in you." Storm's chuckle rumbled and rocked through his chest, and his cock swelled in his jeans. Across from him, Jenna's nipples pebbled against the fabric of her shirt.

"There's a lot you don't know about me, boyfriend."

Playing along, his jaw dropped, feigning shock, horror.

"Stop." Her small fist thumped his chest. "I mean boyfriend as in, hey girlfriend."

Determined not to give her an inch, he frowned, imagined her stripped to her underwear and prayed she wore black lace. And who the fuck was he kidding? If Jen stood in front of him, dressed in Lot Less' bargain polyester, she'd still be the sexiest woman to tread the boards of planet Earth.

"Oh, to hell with it. Let's get fucking wet." Her voice trembled.

And he wanted nothing more than his fingers lathered in soap, gliding across her silky skin, over her navel and through the seam at the top of her thighs. But she had to be certain. Once they opened this gate, for him, it would never close. "Jen?"

He didn't stop her when she wriggled free of his grasp and folded her arms. It pissed him off, that a single fucking word, her name for Christ's sake, shut him out.

His hands caught her hips and pulled her closer. "Don't do this. I want you to be sure, sweetheart." He breathed into her hair. "I'm in. It's no secret." Storm feathered the bridge of her nose with his lips and lifted her onto the second step. "That's better. You will look at me as I show you what you mean to me."

Arms clasped around his neck, her breasts against his chest, she closed her eyes.

"Open your eyes, Jen. No guilt, no pain. Only this." Determined to go slow, he traced the seam between her lips with the tip of his tongue. Licked and nudged until they parted.

If he pushed, he'd taste her heat, erode any excuse, tormenting them both. Instead, he grazed her cheek and chin with his teeth, nipped and sucked across the pulse point at the side of her neck, and whispered how he intended to bring her more pleasure than she ever imagined.

Replacing what she and Rob had was impossible. He got it. The man cornered a huge part of Jen's life, but he hoped, with a fire that threatened to drag his soul straight to hell, she'd give him a chance to love her, too.

"I'm going to carry you upstairs to my shower, turn on the water, and let it run until we're squeaky clean. Then I plan to fuck you all night long. Okay?" He swirled his tongue around the inside of her ear.

"Yes."

"With open eyes, Jen."

"Yes."

A single word, beside her sharp intake of breath, knocked his heart to its knees. His cock swelled, pressed painfully against his zipper. Sweet. Storm scooped her into his arms and took the stairs two at a time and kicked the bathroom door shut behind them.

He surged forward and pressed her back against the wall. His erection pushed against her belly, crying out to be free of his jeans. "Feel me. The chemistry zapping between us when we touch, hell whenever I think of you, and that is every second in a day. It's fucking dynamite."

Chapter Twenty-Four

Storm wasn't wrong. Jenna's mind and body exploded. Knowing she had the power to draw this man to the edge of his control aroused her just as much as the touch of his magic fingers.

Moonlight filtered through the bathroom skylight and carved deep into the perfect angles of his masculine face. His sensuous lips begged for a kiss as the rough tips of his fingers massaged her ears and softly pinched the lobe.

Rob, with a heart larger than a Super Bowl stadium, never wished her to spend the rest of her life alone, insisted she find someone after he was gone. At the time, she wept and told him it wasn't possible even when he insisted. *I need to know you'll be happy.*

But as her body responded to the gentle glide of Storm's fingers caressing her skin, breathing vitality into her body, guilt called her a liar. The impossible had lost its claim on her soul.

"Feel how much I want you, Jen?" Storm whispered in her ear.

"Yes." A moan of betrayal slipped into the room as though it had every right to be there. Heaven help her, but she loved this woman Jen, the inner vixen who grabbed his T-shirt and dragged him closer. Core to core, they fit perfectly. Unashamed, she pleaded for more. Demanded his kiss.

When he molded her palm to the hard bulge pressing against the front of his jeans, blood pounded in her ears, and the tingling at the top of her thighs followed a strangled yes from her lips.

She wanted him now. No more excuses. Lying beneath him on the bed, the floor, the couch. Who cared? Allowing him to touch and taste every, don't miss a freckle, inch of her body.

"Undo my belt," he growled. "Do it now."

If this was a bad idea, her brain should shout louder. Lust running wild in her veins, Jenna gripped the edge of Storm's t-shirt, yanked it over his head and tossed it to the floor. Her face flushed as her pinkie slid beneath the waistband of his jeans and grazed his pubic hair. *Jen, girl, you rock.*

"Fuck, Jen. Keep that up and we won't make it to the soap," he hissed, as he shucked his jeans and kicked them under the sink.

He surged forward and their mouths clashed in a mutual grin. "I'm clean." Except for the dirty thoughts tripping over themselves to put into action.

"Me, too," he said, his eyes the color of clouds before they let loose the rain. "Serious. We get checked."

"Oh." Jenna bit back a smile, realizing his mind was streets ahead of hers. "Good. Oh, my God." She laughed. "Are we really doing this?"

The half-step Storm put between them was enough to send a cloaking chill across her shoulders.

"Tell me you want this, Jen."

"No doubt in my mind." Only half a lie this time, because she figured her head was only a blip behind her heart.

Hands on her hips, Storm narrowed the glacial gap between them, his erection pressing against her pubic bone. Goosebumps erupted on her skin, her pulse roared in her ears, and like a wonton lunatic, up and down, she rubbed her clit against him, like a wonton lunatic chasing release.

***

"That's it, sweetheart." Storm gripped Jen's hips and slowed the rhythm of her ride. "Easy. Take what you need." An agonized growl rumbled in his chest.

Jen's slight frame nestled against his pulsing cock. His control hanging by a thread, he trailed butterfly kisses along her fragile collarbone, over her sternum, to her beautiful breasts.

"Unless I plan on taking that shower fully clothed. I ought to get naked." Jenna shuddered.

"Fuck the shower."

"I love it when you read my mind." A shy smile hovered over the edges of her mouth.

Fucking adorable. "What do you need?" he whispered, willing to do whatever it took to give her pleasure. With every nip, suck, and bite, he planned on proving he wanted more than a quick roll in the sack.

"This. I want this." Jenna palmed her perfect breast and lifted it to his lips. "Suck. Suck hard."

Sweat pricked between the creases on his brow. Bowing his head, Storm licked the pebbled nipple through the thin fabric of her shirt, and pinched the other one, loving it when she winced and smiled.

Her body writhed against his erection, a gasp trembled on her lips. A sound he wanted to hear every day for the rest of his life. Strong fingers pressed into the tender flesh at the base of his skull, encouraging him to do as she demanded and latch on and worship that stiff peak.

Through her jeans, he felt how damp she was as her clit glided along his length. Torture. Fucking bliss. She was his. The truth of it roared from his body.

Storm drank in every one of Jen's sweet sounds and prayed she granted him more than this night. Mesmerized by the need glistening in her eyes, he released her nipple and turned his attention to her other breast. Memorized her sighs, his name on her lips. Perfect.

His mouth took hers, seizing a kiss. Jenna's hand slipped between them again, squeezing his cock with enough force to turn him blind. Sparks ignited at the base of his spine.

Returning the favor, he undid the button on her pants, dragged aside her flimsy underwear, and pinched the swollen numb. Her breath hitched.

"Please," she gasped.

He pushed one finger, then a second, inside her. Appreciating how her sweet sighs turned to guttural moans as she continued to stroke him almost made him come in her hand. Not until she flew apart in his arms.

Storm added another finger, hooked it forward, and found her g-spot. With a low keening, Jen clutched his forearms and arched backward. The back of her head hit the marble tiles. "Easy, lover. I prefer you conscious when you scream my name." He flicked her clit with his thumb.

"Harder." Sharp fingernails dug into his neck.

"Let go, sweetheart. I want to see you come." Storm increased the pace of his fingers moving in and out of her wet heat, driving into her until her mouth opened wide in a silent scream, and she flew over the edge.

Mine. The word took orbit, scaring the shit out of him. Why? He'd wanted Jenna from the moment they met. Insane, if it didn't feel so right. When he married Christine, proud that a woman with her looks bothered to give him the time of day, rookie pride had him believing they were forever.

Once he saw beneath her false eyelashes and fancy clothes, the icing on that cake took less than a month to melt. Beautiful. Sure. But not the perfect someone to spend a lifetime with. Besides, she denied ever saying she wanted kids. A game changer. Despite his job, the weeks missing from home, one day, he believed he'd have a family of his own, two, three kids.

"Is anything wrong?" Jen's arms hung heavy around his neck.

Amazed at where his mind had gone, he gazed into the calm blue eyes of the woman who held his heart, gave him peace. "Never better, Doc." He sighed, content to just hold her. Words hovered on the tip of his tongue as his damn phone chirped.

"Leave it?" she whispered.

The edge of her thumbs stroked his earlobes. "Tempting, but it might be Snake with intel." They had called him before they left the hospital. He bent to pick up his jeans, dragged the phone from the pocket, and hesitated. If she insisted on him ignoring the call, he had no problem running the interruption under the tap.

"Of course. Go ahead." Jenna rubbed the crease between his eyebrows. "I'm not going anywhere."

Storm cupped the back of her head. "Stay close, sweetheart." Her soft curves warmed the chill in his bones. He tilted his head to the side. One last chance to send the call to hell.

"Answer it." She grinned.

"Storm." He trailed the tip of his finger over Jen's shoulder and down her arm.

"It's me, lover."

"Christine?" *What the...speak of the devil.* She hadn't called him in months. "Why the hell are you calling?"

"I need to talk to you. Meet me at our café. Half an hour."

Our café didn't exist, never had, for him, but he knew where she meant. "Okay. Don't be late." He hung up, anger tugging at his gut. Leaving Jenna was the last thing he wanted, but if he didn't show, Christine would keep right on calling. Best to hear her out and set her straight for the last time. In person.

"I'd better check on Tom." Jenna said, her voice flat, as she did up the button of her pants.

"Sure. All good. I have to go out for a while," he said. He finished putting on his pants and pulled a sweatshirt off the hook on the bedroom door.

"I heard."

"Right. It's nothing, Jen." Her body went rigid as he did his best to pull her close. "Won't take long. Then we can..."

"All good," she parroted.

Her squeaky, no big deal tone pissed him off.

"Take all the time you need. I'm exhausted. Probably be asleep by the time you get back. If you're around, I'll see you in the morning."

Say what?

Jenna tucked her shirt into her pants and smoothed the sides of her hair. Lips swollen from his kisses trembled, and her face was too fucking pale. Christine, killer of the afterglow. Damn her.

Jenna followed him to the front door. "Lock up and set the security code." She nodded. He stood outside, kicking the step with the tip of his boot, and waited to hear her do what he asked.

Damn his ex and her lousy timing, but if Jen thought whatever they'd started ten minutes ago had finished, she was mistaken.

Chapter Twenty-Five

Storm rested his elbow on the back of his chair and lunged his right leg for a deep calf stretch. His whole body ached, including his fucking teeth. Way before gramps made his ass a target, he'd hated sitting for too long. He tilted his head sideways. His neck cracked in a zillion places.

Above him, the fluorescent lights buzzed. Time for a switch, plus the walls were begging for a fresh lick of paint.

"Got any gum." Trigger brushed past him.

"Nope". Storm switched legs, noting how he wasn't the only antsy one in the room. Odd, seeing as Trig held Sentinel rank as King of Control. A natural leader, seldom bothered by shit, large or small.

Right now, he'd hold the bottom rank. The soles of his feet itched to head home and sort things out with Jen. Damn his ex for landing in another financial mess and expecting him to fix it. She may not be the woman for him, but she had a knack for pulling his strings. He'd never stand by and see her hurt.

Long stints serving overseas, handling crap for Uncle Sam, weren't the only reasons their marriage failed, although long stints on her own contributed to the reason she self-medicated.

Christine made no attempt to hide the fresh bruises on her face. Why should she? When he saw the handprint curled around her neck, he swore to beat the crap out of her scrawny ass drug dealer, except when he caught up with the dick, he was in worse shape than his ex. For the last time, he paid his ex's debt and warned the fucker to get the hell out of town if he didn't want to end up floating in the Hudson.

It took most of the night to convince Christine to return to rehab. In the end, he packed her bag, half-dragged her to the clinic, and refused to budge until she promised not to take off the minute he left.

Jen feigned sleep when he got home. Understandably pissed at him for taking off, she offered no smile to light up his murky world. It killed him, but he crashed in his own fucking room. Alone. Not what he'd intended. When the boss texted, summoning everyone to this briefing, he'd left without waking her.

Every Sentinel team had assembled in the War Room, been there all day and still no sign of Snake. George crouched at his feet, tongue hanging out the side of his mouth, his wet K9 nose aimed at the ceiling. The dog sniffed and squinted at him. His version of a smile and a wink—Snake must be close.

Storm ran his fingers through the wiry hair on the dog's back. Memories rippled through him of Jen riding his hand, her perfect curves pressed against his body. His phone vibrated in his pocket.

Jenna: *Where r you?*

Storm: *Briefing. Sleep okay last night?*

Jenna: *Yes.*

The muscles across his upper back tightened. With a chuckle, he lifted his right foot onto the seat of the chair. *Not buying it, sweetheart.*

Storm: *Great.*

Trigger nudged his elbow, offering him a stick of his precious gum. "Nah, man. Thanks." Storm stared at the screen, counting the seconds until he saw Jenna and persuaded her to pick up where they left off before Christine rattled his cage.

Storm: *What you doing?*

Jenna: *Packing.*

His foot slipped and his boot thudded onto the floor. The urge to slam his phone at the damn wall roared inside him.

Storm: *You going somewhere?* Dumb fucking question. He followed with, *No* and waited.

Jenna: *We talked about this?*

Sure did, and he thought he made himself pretty damn clear.

Storm: *Not a good idea. Remember?*

A smiley emoji popped up on the screen then his screen turned black. Christine and her shit timing. Storm raked a hand through his hair and faced his team. "The boss can kiss my a..." His blood boiling, he made it to the door as Snake entered.

"Gentlemen. Thanks for coming. Apologies for keeping you." Arms folded, Snake leaned against the front of his desk and stared him down.

Okay, the tone and timing of his aborted exit wasn't great, but Jenna freaked him out with her leaving crap. Clenching his teeth, he lowered his gaze.

"What do you need, boss?" Trig asked, elbows on his knees.

Snake siphoned a long breath through his nose. Havoc followed with a grunt, while Trigger cleared his throat. Winter shrugged. *Dammit. Out with it.* Whatever lay tucked between the pages of that manila folder in the boss' hand wasn't Sam's shopping list.

Storm scratched behind George's ears. *When tested, keep your hands active and your mouth shut.*

"We have new intel." Snake opened his file and pulled out a sheet of paper. "Hawke shared a lead on our gunman, a.k.a. our hit-and-run driver."

Storm felt his switch flip to on for the second time in ten minutes. "And?"

"Yesterday evening, she alerted me to a connection between your last mission in Somalia. Five seconds before I entered the room, she confirmed that link."

Once again, the boss pinned him in place with a look.

"Congratulations, Storm. You shot Hassan's grandfather."

"My ass."

"Precisely." Trig smirked.

Mother fucker. His blood pressure soared to max and kept right on truckin'.

Snake drilled his fingers on the desk. "Hawke believes the death of granddad, the shooter, and the girl's hit and run are connected."

"Name's Tina," Storm grumbled. No professional distancing. This was personal. With a huff, George stood and wagged his tail. The dog had his back.

"Apologies. Tina's murder."

Storm returned the boss' nod. Hassan was out for revenge—his damn fault. People he cared most about targeted because his trigger finger twitched. Jenna had a backbone made of A-grade titanium, but she and Tom had endured way too much shit in their lives. And listening to him, trusting her son's safety to Dexter, had got Tina killed. CCTV proved how easily the boy avoided the ex-Marine.

"Said it before. One giant clusterfuck, that entire mission." Havoc stated.

"That it was." Winter patted his knee and tilted his chin at George.

George took the hint and padded over to share some love.

"Yeah, man, starting with your fucking bed," Trig chuckled.

"Gentlemen." Snake rolled his eyes. "Your attention. Hawke confirmed Hassan knows Storm shot granddad and has issued a seek and destroy order."

"Way to go, hero." Trigger raised his hand for a high five.

Storm gave him a one-finger salute. As if putting Tom, Jen, and his Sentinel brothers in danger wasn't enough, he sensed those bonus steak knives aimed at his chest. Sure enough, there was more.

Snake continued. "Storm is Hassan's first, but not his only target. Anyone he considers family is on the man's hit list."

"Bullshit. How did he find out who we are, where we live?" Fucking terrified, Storm's voice cracked.

"Good question. Hawke's working on it."

Everyone knew the computer geek's abilities. A waste of effort asking her to name her sources or where she got her intel, but her contacts saved their asses on a regular basis.

Winter shrugged. "So, what are we gonna do about it, boss?"

"What we're trained to do. We finish this. Use everything in our power, and arsenal, to find the fucker and put an end to him before anyone else gets hurt."

"I'm in." As one, the team spoke.

First, he needed eyes on Tom and Jen. Right fucking now. At the door, he swung his body to face Snake.

The boss nodded. "Go."

Trigger grinned. Winter grunted. They understood, and if Storm had his way, his team brothers wouldn't wait long before he confirmed his family unit with a ring on Jen's finger.

"Thanks, boss." Storm clenched his fists and prayed they were too busy throwing fruit loops at each other to finish packing. That they weren't out there alone. No matter what she said, snow would fall in July before he surrendered her safety, failed to protect her. *With my bare hands, if needed.*

The journey back to Brooklyn went by in a blur as he worked to control the turmoil in his gut. He wasn't beyond tying Jen and the kid to his bed, if that's what it took to keep them safe. Thank God, he still had half a brain, the better half that warned don't push too hard.

Standing in his hallway, Storm softened his features. A mask to hide the turmoil still seething inside him. "Jen?" Storm kicked the door shut and hit each room. He didn't need the shiver down his spine telling him they had left. He bounded upstairs and headed straight to her bedroom.

The closet was open, hangers swiped clean. *Fuck me.* Gone.

Chapter Twenty-Six

As the light turned green, Jenna eased her foot onto the accelerator and shot through the intersection. After living in Manhattan for close to a year, she ought to be used to the traffic. Getting anywhere in Manhattan always took longer than she expected.

The streets groaned under the never-ending weight of cars, buses, bikes, anything on wheels, thundering through the city, obliterating any chance of landing her backside on a sofa soon. The wind whistled through the gaps in the window seal. The wipers worked overtime trying to sweep of the leaves plastered to the windshield.

Tom and Storm hated her working late. The latter for very different reasons, she suspected. Not that it mattered anymore. Her body reacted to the memory of his hands working her body in the bathroom, and she'd be kidding herself if she denied wondering what tricks he had in his bedroom arsenal. *You'll never know.*

Because there was nothing ex about Christine. After she called, he didn't hesitate to go meet her. And she hated herself for feeling pushed aside. Easy to forget. Knowing she'd messed up. Again. Lying in her room, she'd heard him come home and the door creak open, but she pretended to be asleep.

At work, she had zero problem with making the hard call. Not so easy in her personal life, but tonight, she planned on packing their bags and heading home. No more excuses.

Ugh. The back of her throat felt like sandpaper. Keeping one eye on the road, she shuffled under the papers on the passenger seat, searching for her drink bottle. Still full. Untouched from when she filled it that morning. And when had she last eaten anything except crackers and chocolate? Lately, she heaved at the thought of real food.

Suddenly, a bike messenger with a death wish came out of nowhere and zigzagged in front of her. *Shivers, slow down.* Her knuckles turned white from grasping the steering wheel. Did the driver who killed Tina become distracted as he sped to the next red light? Except Tom insisted he headed straight for them. Murdered his friend.

Luckily, outside Sentinel, the parking angels were on her side, and a spot materialized. Jenna swung to the curb and backed into the space. Crooked, but she had no energy to do better.

With a groan, she rested her forehead on the steering wheel, took a sec to catch her breath, and blinked moisture into her gritty eyeballs. While she sucked in oxygen, her mind inevitably drifted to Storm's incredible body. It was fast becoming a habit.

Clothed, his physique was impressive. Wide shoulders, narrow waist, muscular legs. Tick, tick, tick. Her fingers failed to close around his thick cock. Jenna groaned and squinted at the misty rain shrouding the sidewalk and did her best to focus on parts of Storm's anatomy that didn't make her wet. His intense, penetrating gaze. Piercing eyes the color of swirling smoke that cut through her crap, straight to her soul. *Oh, for goodness' sake.* This Jen girl better get back in her box.

"Hey, lady. You leaving?" A man yelled from the window of a passing car.

Jenna hauled her tired body onto the sidewalk. "Sorry. Won't be long. I'll be gone by the time you circle the block," she shouted over the wind.

"Great. Thanks."

She returned his smile as the guy drove off and she pounded Sentinel's entry code with her numb finger. As the door swung open, she almost collided with Sam.

"Ah, I was hoping I'd catch you." Sam said.

"Really? I didn't realize you were coming in today." Jenna glanced over her friend's shoulder, a rush of heat warming her cheeks, as she half expected Snake and the rest of the team to exit the War Room. With little notice, the team often went wheels up to save the world.

"Had some stuff to do in town, so I thought I'd stop by and say hello. Forgot you were at the Hub. I was just leaving, but when are you going to let that amazing boy of yours come stay with me at the kennels? I need help setting up a new scent trail."

Jenna laughed and hooked her hand through Sam's arm. Tom loved hanging out with her and his fur buddies. Time away might take his mind off Tina. No chance of Snake allowing him to hide in his room playing computer games.

And until this business with shooters and hit-and-run drivers got sorted, she'd feel a lot better knowing her son was out of the city. Out of harm's way. Back at her place, having only herself to look after would make life a lot easier.

Jenna tugged Sam's forearm. "I'll talk to him. I'm sure he'd love being with you, and he's on school break starting tomorrow. Come and talk to me while I grab my papers. Haven't got long. There's a poor guy circling the block, wanting my spot."

Too busy to look up as they passed, Linda sat at reception filing her nails. They were amazing. A fact all the girls agreed on. Maggie, Winter's wife, had plucked up courage and asked her how she kept them looking perfect. Got a bit more than she bargained for when Linda put her on a supervised routine.

Jenna shut the door of her clinic as a wave of nausea gripped her stomach. The room tilted sideways. Placing her hand on her desk, she took a deep breath and steadied herself.

"Easy girl. Sit down for a sec." Sam led her to a chair. "Haven't eaten today, I bet." She shook her head. "No water, either. Doc?" Sam fished a glass from under the clinic sink, filled it, and handed it to her.

"Thanks."

"What's going on? I heard Storm left the team briefing earlier to find you. You miss each other?" She tilted her head sideways.

"Really? Must have missed him." Jenna stared at the photo of Tom and Rob on her desk.

"Okay. Come on, Jenna. What gives?" Sam threw her hands in the air as though she expected bloody intervention from the divine.

The glass jittered. "What gives? You are kidding me."

Sam smacked her forehead with the heel of her hand. "No. Maybe I'm a complete tit, but I'm worried about you. And you know me. Not the most tactful human."

"True." Jenna grinned. "I'm not ill, but I do want to stick my head under the sheets and stay in bed until they find that sodding shooter and the maniac who killed Tina."

"And we will. Snake has the entire team working on it. Surely, Storm can help with the whole under-the-sheet activities."

Sam flashed her the veteran warrior face with a wink. "Thanks for offering to let Tom come and stay. I'll miss him, but the idea is perfect."

"Believe me, our pleasure. Talking about finding our fucking villains, if Storm doesn't stop attacking the carpet in the War Room with his enormous feet, we'll dock his pay to buy a new one. That soldier can pace a marathon in under an hour. Is it true you're dead set on leaving his and going back to your place?"

"Already done. Packed this morning. I miss my space, and we can't stay with him forever." The shift of her voice up an octave made her ears hurt. "Besides, he has a wife?"

"No. They're divorced as in end of, no longer."

"Wrong. Well, half-wrong. Christine called last night. After we—" She bit her tongue. *Damn it.*

"'Bout time."

Jenna groaned. "No. Not all the way," she bit back, feeling like she must have hopped a time travel capsule and landed back in high school. "Anyway. It doesn't matter." She clasped her hands and straightened her spine. "What Storm does with Christine, or any other woman, is his business."

"True. Except you two have been shaking your tail feathers at each other since you arrived in the good ole U. S. of A. Any fool with eyesight has clocked your chemistry. The way Storm tracks your every move borders on the obscene. What's more, I'd bet our next pedicure that he wants more from you than getting you naked."

"Like what?"

"Don't be fucking coy. He's enthralled. Possibly thinking there's a chance at a relationship lurking in his future." She swirled her hands around an imaginary fortune teller's globe.

"Hilarious. He knows I'm not interested in anything serious. Pretty sure, it's never again for me. You understand. You were there when the whole Baxter crap went down."

"I was, and I get it. Cock shy. But Storm is not Baxter." She shrugged. "Talk to him, Jenna."

"There's nothing to say. We're friends." Jenna didn't miss Sam's smirk. "His ex, remember?"

"Ex! Bingo. You said it, and at the risk of sounding like I've fallen into the never-ending story, let me repeat. Talk to him. Dumb move leaving his place, if you ask me."

"Argh! You drive me nuts. And I'm not asking."

"Yeah, yeah, yeah. And you love me."

Jenna laughed, rose from her chair, and threw her arms around her friend's neck. "That bit you got right," she muttered, sniffing back a tear.

A sharp knock stopped them from falling into a blithering clinch. Arms folded, Linda stood in the doorway.

"There's a woman at my desk insisting on seeing Jenna. I said you were unavailable, but she's not listening. Sat her ass down and refuses to budge."

"Fuck, Linda. You are Sentinel's Guardian of the Gate. Deal with it." Sam ordered and scraped her fingers through her hair.

Linda turned and stabbed her finger toward her desk. "That woman's a psycho. So, unless Snake plans on paying me danger money, she's yours."

Like a kid with no fear, Linda squared off with Sam. Seizing the opportunity, Jenna bowed her head and swiped away her tears with the back of her hand. If Linda saw her upset, she'd never hear the end of it. "What's her name?"

"Flores. Hispanic."

"Yay high, with a hemangioma." Jenna touched her cheek.

Sam raised an eyebrow and waved a tissue in front of her. *Traitor.*

"If that means she has a brown patch on the side of her face. Yeah. You gonna deal with her, or not?"

Sam sailed past Linda. "Both of you stay here. I'll see what she wants."

"No, wait. I'll go. It's Tina's mum." Jenna dodged them both and marched into the hall.

"I'll be here when you're finished." Sam quipped.

"Oh, no. Our conversation is over." Jenna drove as much steel into her voice as possible, given her empty stomach, and glanced at her watch. "Go home. I'll talk to Tom and call you tonight about him coming for a visit."

At reception, Jenna sat next to the woman, doing her best to disappear into her chair. Bloodshot eyes peered at her from the head sunk between hunched shoulders. "Hi, Mrs. Flores. How are you? I'm sorry I haven't come to visit?" She was ashamed to admit it out loud.

"*Por favor*. Please. I didn't know where else to go. I need help." Her whole body trembled.

Chapter Twenty-Seven

As much as Jenna pleaded with herself to keep it together, her skin crawled with Mrs. Flores' grief. Her bone deep pain she understood. Listening to Tina's mum reminded her of the weeks following Rob's death when her despair had been contagious.

She'd spent hours spent begging, senselessly requesting the universe for answers. Lost sleep. Didn't eat. Her heart kept beating only because Tom needed her. Mrs. Flores had no family and now she'd lost her daughter. Jenna couldn't get her grief-stricken face out of her head, stop it from occupying the entire space in front of her.

No wonder she didn't hear Winter enter Snake's office. But then, built like Sherman tanks, Sentinel men had a talent for moving their size twelve, flat feet with Ninja-like silence.

"Good morning, Jenna. The Boss sends his apologies. Delayed uptown, so you've got me."

"No problem. I can wait until he gets back to the office." Winter had given her an excuse to rethink the whole thing. After all, she didn't want to waste more of their time. They were working on trying to find the driver, but Sentinel had more than her tiny corner of the world to save.

She should go with Mrs. Flores to the police and give them a nudge. Kick their arses, more like it. Jenna practically jumped out of her chair.

"Sit, Jenna. Please." Winter nodded at the chair. "Snake, anyone here, knows it must be important if you asked for a meeting. Come on. Share a coffee with me, and tell me what's on our mind?"

Knowing he wouldn't let it go, she sat. He did the same, settling in behind Snake's desk. Jenna had never known her colleagues not to be on board, at any suspicion a person needed help. Prepared to lay down their lives to keep the vulnerable safe.

Their last mission almost got Storm killed. A knot formed in her throat as she recalled how she begged him to take a painkiller. That time, he'd been lucky, a graze to his perfect backside. What next? A bullet to the head? An IUD? Her medical colleague at Sentinel Security in London had seen his best friend die in his arms. Jenna shuddered, imagining Storm miles away, bleeding out and not being able to help him.

Winter rubbed his palms together. "Jenna? What's it gonna be? Coffee?" His nose twitched. "Tea?"

Relaxing a little at the hint of the magic brew, she grinned. "No, thank you." Ever since talking with Mrs. Flores, her head hadn't stopped pounding. Bordering on hysterical, before Jenna managed to calm her, Tina's mum had exploded with questions. Police kept putting her off. Why did they keep telling her they had no leads on the hit-and-run driver?

Winter picked up the phone on his desk. "Last chance, Doc".

"Okay. A tea, with milk."

Winter smiled and pressed the intercom button. "Linda. One black coffee, and a tea with milk, please. Thanks."

Jenna rolled her lips and shook her head. "Oh, no. Stupid. I thought you were making them. Linda's up to her eyeballs in work." She said, dreading another of Linda's, this isn't what I'm paid for, rants.

Winter nodded. "Second thoughts. Cancel those." He rose from his chair and towered over the desk. "Don't move, Doc. I have no problem making the drinks. Sugar?" He winked.

The kindness Maggie loved about her man twinkled in his brown eyes. "One, please." Jenna smiled. While he was gone, she went over the speech she'd prepared for Snake, the justification for Sentinel to do more. Push for answers for Mrs. Flores.

In record time, Winter returned and slipped a blank piece of paper under the steaming mug he placed on the desk in front of her. "Sorry, we're out of sugar, but I raided the last of the Oreos in the cookie barrel."

That small gesture crushed her. Tears, banked behind her eyeballs for the past few hours, streamed over her cheeks. "I..."

Winter cupped her hands in his. "Jenna. Look at me."

"What the hell is going on?" Storm growled, anger firing behind his smoky gray eyes.

Terrific. Crazy Ninja Two had tip-toed into the room. Giant steps from happy, Storm's eyebrows steepled against the deepening lines on his forehead. While she swallowed a few times, sorting out whether she wanted to hug or slap him, Winter shook his hand.

"Hey, bro. Take a seat. Doc has a problem."

"Problem?" Storm switched his hand from Winter's grasp to her shoulder.

Before the tirade of his texts last night when he found she'd meant what she said and gone home, Jenna might have appreciated the warmth of his touch. The gentle squeeze of his strong fingers. That same ordinary soul may have relaxed, but no-stress moments had not found her in a long time.

Chapter Twenty-Eight

J en's shoulder trembled under Storm's touch. He'd come on too strong, but he couldn't help himself. After he realized she'd left, rage, raw and dark, overrode any sense of reason. Prepared to drag her kicking and screaming back to his if he had to, whatever it took, to keep her and Tom safe, he'd driven to her place.

For several hours he froze his balls off sitting in his car outside, sending a bunch of dumb texts pleading with her to let him in, to come the fuck home. Giving her space, at least until he calmed down and have a calm conversation was for the best.

She probably wouldn't believe him, but he hadn't stalked her to Sentinel. He had to do a final weapon check before they went wheels up for Somalia. Should have guessed, the second the toe of his boot landed inside the office, he'd never escape Jen's magnetic orbit.

Seeing Winter's paws on Jen ignited his very short fuse. The green-eyed monster dug his claws in deep, and he wanted to tear his bud apart. Not good. Losing control jeopardized the bond he and his Sentinel brothers relied on to ensure they all came home in one piece from a mission.

Around Jenna, he lost all sense of boundary, and up until now, he had never had call to be jealous. In past relationships, if eyes wandered, fair enough, sayonara. No hard feelings.

And what was with her tears? If Winter had made her cry, brother or not, bones would break. His gaze scanned the empty seat next to her, but he stayed standing. Raising his chin at Winter, he repeated his goddam question. "Problem?"

Jenna shrugged his hand from her shoulder.

"Chill bro. Can I get you a beverage, tea, coffee?" His teammate headed for the door.

"No, Wendy Waitress, I don't want a fucking beverage." *Jerk off.* He wanted answers. Like, why hadn't Jenna come to him? Why did she run? Storm kneeled beside her and lightly placed his palm on her knee.

Despite the dark circles under her eyes, the messed hair, her uncrushable, inner beauty shone bright. "What's happening, Jen? I am sorry. My texts were *dumb, immature,* overkill, but please don't shut me out, sweetheart."

"I'm fine. It's…"

"Tom? He's okay?" His gut played leapfrog with his throat. If anything has happened to the kid.

"No. I mean, yes. He left for Sam and Snake's after breakfast. It's Tina's mum. She was here. Christ, Storm. She's at her wit's end, begged me to help her find the hit-and-run driver." Jenna sighed. "What could I say? I know Sentinel is doing all it can, but I just wanted to speak with Snake. See if he could tell me anything more to reassure Mrs. Flores. If it were Tom lying on a slab in the morgue, I'd…"

Storm's heart plummeted to his boots. "Easy, Doc." He gently uncurled Jen's clenched fist and stroked the inside of her wrist. "You should have told me." His voice deepened, the words sounding like an accusation.

Jenna snatched her fingers from his hand and rested them on her chest.

"In your time, sweetheart. We're not going anywhere." He flicked his chin at Winter, who nodded.

"I intended to call you, but you have done enough for Tom and me. Besides…"

"The texts. I get it. Like I said, I'm an idiot."

"No. You have a ton of stuff on your mind. Christine?"

Out of the corner of his eye, he saw Winter's jaw drop. *Yeah, yeah. Later.*

Jenna stood. "Anyway, I rang Sam. She set up this meeting with

Snake."

"True, bro. I'm the stand-in." Winter added.

He was so focused on Jen chewing her bottom lip, he barely heard his teammate. "It's bull, thinking you're bothering me. And imagining shit going down with me and Christine is plain dumb." *Dammit.* "Sorry." The pressure to get the hell out of there before he said more shit made him sweat. He rose from his knees at the same time Winter sprang to his feet and barricaded the exit.

"Take no notice of doofus, Jenna. Go on." Winter encouraged her with a wave of his hand.

"The police told Mrs. Flores the case is closed, and they won't re-open it unless there is more evidence. Unbelievable." she blurted and threw her arms wide. "Tom insists, after the driver hit Tina, he meant to swing round and come for him." Her voice hitched. "Don't say it. Yes, teenagers are drama queens, but if he is sure that's what happened, I believe him.

Son of a bitch. Storm curled his hands into fists. "Hey. We agree. This sucks. But we know what's going on."

Jenna tilted head. "What do you mean?" Jenna sprang to her feet and threw her weight behind a punch to his chest. "Don't look at me as though I've grown an extra set of ears. What's going on? My kid, Tina's mum, they are a mess. What are you two not telling me?"

Storm blocked Jenna's second swing by grabbing her wrist and pulling it to her side.

"Let go of me." Jenna pivoted and reached for the door handle with her free hand.

Damn. Her eyes, swimming in pain, pierced his soul. He released her.

"Goodnight, Winter," she said and opened the door.

His heart pounded at the thought of losing her again. "No. You're not going anywhere. Sit." *What the hell was he doing?* Fury pulsed off her in waves, along with bone crushing hurt.

"Jenna. I'm not sure if you've met Hawke?" Winter drawled, as though he was asking if she wanted one of his coffees.

"I have. Go on."

Storm offered no resistance when she pushed past him and flopped into her chair. "Hawke's been tapping her sources. Contacts. We now know that the shooting, and Tina's accident, are likely connected to our recent mission."

"When you got shot?" Her breath hitched.

Maybe there was hope for him yet.

"Please, Storm. Tell me this isn't about revenge."

Smart woman. Christine was the least of his fucking worries. The bottom dropped out of his world, knowing his next sentence had the power to kill any chance of a future with Jen.

"Oh, God. That's it. Sentinel upset some maniac in Africa, and now he's after me. Tom. You should have told me as soon as you heard? I thought we were friends."

"We are." Storm closed his huge hand over the tiny one clamped to the front of his shirt with the power of an alligator bite. For the first time in his life, he had no clue what to do. How to fix this. How to stop the pain slicing through every organ in his body.

"To be fair." Winter intervened. "As you know, Doc, we never include civilian non-combat personnel in full mission briefings for their safety. Although, I'm sure Maggie will be with you on this one." His voice faded.

"You think? If you are serious, and want to protect me, Tom, and Mrs. Flores, don't we deserve the entire story? To understand what we're up against."

"Of course." Storm mumbled.

Winter lifted his chin. "I'll leave you to it."

And with that, his teammate fled. *Thanks.*

"Just how much danger are we in?" This time, when Jenna's tears fell, Storm wrapped her in his arms and pressed her cheek to his chest. "I will tell you everything, Jen. Over something stronger than a cup of coffee and food. But first, let's go somewhere. Anywhere? We both need to eat."

"No. I want to know. Now."

The fact she was still in his arms gave him strength. "Okay. I killed a man. The wrong man. Kind of." Jenna shook her head and groaned. Damn, he was terrible at this.

"Bilal Hassan. A butcher. That mission in Somalia. We had orders to retrieve and secure him for interrogation." Jen spun her finger in a circle.

Shit. Get on with it. "Hassan wasn't there. His father was. Old, but not innocent. Pop had a stranglehold on a kid, a boy, using him as a shield. I didn't hesitate. I did what needed to be done and took care of the threat. Can't lie to you, sweetheart. I'd do it again."

Storm caught Jenna's chin between his thumb and forefinger. "Hey, he shot me in the ass, remember?" He half-smiled. A pathetic attempt to chase the darkness from her eyes. A void he understood and never wanted her anywhere near.

"My turn to be sorry," she whispered.

The light touch of her fingers on his cheek burned, branded him as hers. "Please, Jen. Come home with me. I will keep you safe. Trust me." He eased her away from his chest, prepared to sink to his knees again. Beg, if that's what it took for her to say yes.

Chapter Twenty-Nine

Jenna's anger melted as she stared into Storm's eyes. Gray as the ocean on a sunless day. She ran the tips of her fingers over the bridge of his nose and along the lines etched across his forehead.

Going home with him, picking up where they left off only hours ago. She should, but how could she resist? Easy. Right this minute, she wanted to murder him. He'd kept stuff from her, but if she hadn't taken the coward's way out and left, would he have told her? That inkling of doubt told her everything. Neither of them fully trusted the other.

"Jen?" Storm's jaw ticked.

"Okay. Food sounds good. Somewhere quiet where we can talk?" This wasted energy building a wall between them had to stop.

"I know a place, Doc. Rug up. It's cold outside."

He draped his scarf around her neck and pulled it snug beneath her chin. The smile softening his mouth made her heart swell. "Okay. My car's out back. I'll follow you."

"Can't let you do that, sweetheart."

His chin dropped, bringing his eyes level with hers.

"Dex will bring it round to mine later."

His tone irked, but the danger was real, so she counted her heartbeats as they walked to his car and kept her mouth shut.

Storm opened her door, circled her waist with his capable hands, and lifted her into her seat. Pointless refusing the macho move. Her body, a swift learner, enjoyed the warmth of his body grazing her skin. Heat coursed along her inside thighs.

Storm closed the door and moved around front to the driver's side.

"Where are we going?" she asked more to make conversation. A quiet place in Manhattan didn't exist.

"You'll see. Close your eyes. I'll wake you when we're there."

His tone irritated the nagging uncertainty in her brain. Unsure if she was doing the right thing, Jenna yanked on her seat belt and faced him. "I'm not a child, and this is not a date. After the bomb you dropped at Sentinel, I want..." The tip of Storm's fingers brushed her lips.

"Answers. A proper apology. I haven't forgotten, but we're both exhausted. Rest while you can."

Jen shifted in her seat. He must have seen her earful speech about women and infantilization coming, because his palms flew to the front of his chest, and he leaned against the window. "Okay. Sorry. Maybe I should have said, dead on your feet, you've never looked more stunning. Except that bayonet gleam in your baby blues says I'd face a slow and excruciatingly painful death."

"You got that right. Just drive, for God's sake." Not surprisingly, she couldn't keep her eyes open. As they exited the Belt and headed onto Ocean Parkway, she woke with a start. By the time she'd wriggled out of her slump and loosened Storm's scarf, he had pulled into the parking lot and turned off the engine.

"Hope you're hungry." He winked.

With a huff, she straightened her spine. Her head crashing against the roof of his car made for a less than graceful exit. The Cyclone fairground ride loomed in the distance against the darkening sky. It got dark early this time of year.

"This way." Storm locked his car and grabbed her hand.

A few minutes later, the unmistakable green and yellow awning of New York's iconic restaurant chain, a Coney Island landmark, stared at her from across the street. "Nathan's? You're taking me for a hot dog? Quiet?" She hooked air quotes around the last word. "It's packed and loud.

"Okay, it's a stretch. But the boardwalk, the water is right there."

He squinted, as though he saw the perfect spot in the distance. Storm grabbed her hand and tugged her into the restaurant. "What's your poison?"

She laughed. "Indeed. These critters have enough salt in them to give me a coronary before we set one foot on that sand.

"No problem. Remember? I am checked-off proficient in mouth-to-mouth."

Jenna punched his upper arm. Impact nil, as her fist rebounded off his solid bicep. "Go on then. Make mine a Chili Cheese Dog, with all the trimmings."

Storm gulped. "You sure about that, Doc?"

The chill when he let go of her hand was unexpected. "Sure am." Jenna perched on a stool by the window. "Don't forget the fries and a pickle." His head cocked to one side. "And if I'm doing this, add a coke. I remember Sam saying they sell chocolate covered frozen bananas around here somewhere, too. Dessert?" When he turned green, she let out a satisfied, "Yes."

***

"Here. Hold this." Storm handed Jenna the takeout and smoothed a place for them in the sand. She didn't need his help, but he grabbed her hand and lowered her to sit beside him. Anything to touch her. A part of him needing to make sure she hadn't taken off while he was ordering food.

Jenna slid her arm through his and when her body relaxed against his side, his world saw daylight. Until she trembled and his senses shot to high alert. "What is it? The dog can't be that bad." He stared at her Chili Cheese monster. "Is it?"

"No. It's, er, tasty."

Jenna licked her lips and his cock took notice. "Pretty, right?" He stared out at the Atlantic, trying to get his arousal under control.

She shook with laughter and jabbed him with her finger. Storm hung his head. In the past, his little boy lost look slayed the ladies. Made them putty in his hands. Never her.

"Sorry. I shouldn't laugh, but if you asked me to write a speech for you, I doubt the word pretty would fall from my pen." She squeezed his arm and hooked her chin over his shoulder.

Hanging onto the horizon, the sun sank behind the purple cloud. "Okay, smarty. I'll have you know I aced English. I have the vocabulary of a poet." He smiled and stared at the sinking ball of light, afraid if he shifted, he'd sever the moment.

"Again, I'm sorry. It is pretty." She pecked his neck.

The direct hit on the pulse point stirred him into action. Storm leaned his forehead against hers. "You're right, I shouldn't have waited. No excuses. I should have banged on your door until you let me in."

"Yes. Promise me you won't keep things from me, Storm. We have to work together on this."

"It's a vow, sweetheart." Hell, if she asked, he'd swear it on his team's survival. "There's something else I need to tell you."

"What?"

Wide eyes searched his face. *Damn.* Storm blew gently on Jen's flushed cheek and grinned. Nothing scary unless you considered him losing his freaking mind dangerous. He sucked in a breath and dived in. "I love you, Jen. I was pretty sure the second Sam introduced us. Impossible. Crazy. True. Although, I admit, kissing you before we made it to first base was a mistake. Should have waited."

"Love? That's a poetry book gem," she muttered. "Falling in love is a huge risk, no matter how long you've known someone. Takes courage. Not sure I can do it again, even though a roller coaster ride with you is tempting." Jenna glanced at the Cyclone. The huge metal struts turned black as the sun disappeared. "Can you hang on for a slow ride?" she asked.

His turn to laugh. "Sure, sweetheart. You take all the goddam time you need. Not going anywhere."

"Take me home, Storm. As pretty as this sunset is, I'm freezing."

Music to his fucking ears. He scooped a trace of mustard from the corner of her mouth with his thumb. "Does this mean you'll stay at mine? At least until this is over?" he added, although he planned on loving her so hard she'd never want to leave.

Their eyes locked, and his stomach flipped. Cool air blowing off the water shimmered through her hair. Lifting her chin with his finger, he brushed her lips with mouth. The growl rumbling in his chest mingled with her low moan.

"Yes. I'll stay. On one condition."

Jen's eyes sparkled. "Name it." Storm stuffed the used napkins into his pocket and tightened his grip around her waist.

"We try sharing a bed."

Her cheeks flushed, and that was it. He scooped his free hand under her bent legs and stood with her in his arms. "Done. That it?"

"Yes. Oh, and I think the bin is over there." She squeezed his pocket.

Her breasts rubbed against his chest as she pointed over his shoulder, and his dick twitched with appreciation. "Fuck, the bin." If he gave Jen time to think, she might change her mind, and he wanted her in his home, exploring his bed.

"You can't drive with this." Her hands skirted across his erection to his other pocket. "Mustard stains," she squealed.

"Okay, easy." Spinning on his heel, he high tailed it to the bin and tossed in the garbage.

"And put me down before you drop me. I was too heavy before that chili dog." Her soft breasts jiggling against his sternum.

"No way in hell. Vehicle in sight." He nipped her ear.

"Ouch. Animal."

"Oh, sweetheart. You should know by now. I love a challenge." Beside the car, he lowered Jenna until the tips of her toes hovered over the sidewalk. "Thank you."

"For what?" Her warm breath spiraled in the frosty air.

"Your trust."

Chapter Thirty

Jenna's heart swelled. Love. The word had tripped over Storm's tongue with an ease she desperately wished to return. A simple word—a new world for her and Tom. Deep down, did she have the strength to honor his offer and commit to everything he deserved?

One foot between her thighs, he pinned her to the door with his forearm. A strong, firm grip, but loose enough to jerk free if she wanted. She did not want. Instead, Jenna scanned his face. Tiny beads of sweat sat on the creases above his eyebrows.

To hell with slow. It didn't matter how much her rational self worried her ear, her vitals skyrocketed every time she imagined what she'd like to do with him in bed. *Clothes off.* Her skin was on fire. First came the scarf he wound around her neck earlier.

Next, her fingers tugged at the buttons on his coat, easing it over his shoulders and sliding it down his arms. It fell to the floor. A hint of a dare lurked behind his sexy silver gaze.

Storm's hand circled her throat and eased her against the wall. When his lips brushed the sensitive spot below her ear, the hairs on her forearms rose to attention and clicked their heels.

Their breath came in short pants, echoing through the hallway, as though they'd run a marathon from the car to the door. When his fingers released her throat and stroked her collarbone, she leaned into his body, quivering with anticipation.

Sparks of electricity zapped every nerve in her body. Intoxicated by the warm breath, the soft growls coming from his mouth, her knees shook.

Her palm was too small to span his thick neck, so she dug her nails into his skin and explored the crease of his mouth with her tongue.

"Christ, Jen. Bedroom. Yes?" He lifted his head and smiled.

Storm's mouth trembled against hers. Passion did that. Short phrases stood for sentences. Single words read like a novel. She nodded and ran for the stairs.

"Need the words, sweetheart."

Funny. He looked lost, standing below her. Heart beating like a metronome gone mad, she reached for his hand. "Yes. Hurry." Her breath fractured.

***

Swallowing the stairs three at a time, Storm chased Jenna's fingers up the stairs and into his bedroom.

Standing beside the bed, a mischievous glint in her eye, she looked vulnerable, drop dead gorgeous, all at the same time, dressed in her parka, and the warm boots tickling knees he couldn't wait to worship. "Coat, off."

Jenna's eyes skittered over his face. Curious? Anxious? *Fuck.* Did she think there was a right way to get naked? "I got you, sweetheart. Tell me what you need."

Her gaze hit the safe zone of his damn floor, and his heart lurched. "Oh, no." He curled his hands around her slim fingers and brought them to his lips. "Don't run. Please."

He had to make her understand. On the beach, he meant what he said. If it took the rest of his life, he'd convince her. But conflicting emotions rode the hitch in her breath and his heart stopped. Seeing Jen every day had become the reason it beat, but what if the past made a future impossible? *What if there is no us?*

"Kiss me." Jen whispered in his ear.

With his heart kickstarted, layers of winter clothing danced with their laughter. Sweaters, pants, underwear. The fucking lot soared over their heads and scattered over the floorboards. Naked and shivering, they linked hands.

"Warm me up." Jenna brushed her breasts over the hairs on his chest.

"Hell, sweetheart. How long have you been the sexiest woman on two legs?" High school, corny, but the sight of blood rushing to her cheeks, that crimson flush, made it worthwhile.

One arm under her knees, the other around her waist, he scooped her off her feet and tossed her on the bed. Her breasts jiggled and his cock jumped. "Scoot over." Grabbing the edge of the duvet, he pulled it over her shoulders. "Warmer?"

Her eyes flickered closed. Intense heat pooled at his tailbone as licked and nipped from her nose to her plush pink lips. "Open your mouth."

"If I must."

"Believe it, sweetheart." Riding a long sigh, a playfulness flashing in her eyes, Jen did as he asked and more. She captured his tongue and sucked him deeper into her heat.

Jenna cared for him. The fact shone from her hazel eyes and sang from her soft moans. If anything happened to this amazing woman, he wouldn't survive. "Let me love you." He dipped his head and caught her nipple between his teeth.

Caught on a breath, her back arched. Storm moved over her and sucked.

"Oh God, yes."

His cock agreed. Her skin smelled amazing, and she tasted better than that nectar the gods drank by the gallon. His belly tightened each time she gasped, his balls pulsed in sync with her sighs. Stretching an arm from underneath the cover, he switched on the bed lamp.

"Storm?"

"Easy. I don't want to miss a single inch." Her nails bit into the top of his shoulders. Who cared? *Mark me.* He nipped her ivory skin and circled her rosy nipple with his tongue.

As close to bliss as any man would ever get, pins and needles zinged the length of his spine and hit the base of his skull with the power of a scud missile.

He sucked and rolled the other nub between his thumb and finger, lavishing attention on both as she bucked underneath him.

"Storm, I want..." Jen moaned. Her small fingers found his cock and stroked him from base to tip.

Jesus. "What? Tell me." In danger of exploding, if he didn't get inside her soon, he licked and sucked his way across her flat belly and to the dark hair between her legs.

Using his shoulders, he parted her thighs and dragged his tongue over her clit, then pushed inside her.

"Oh, God." Jen's hips writhed against his face.

He worked his tongue in and out, memorizing memorized every sigh and groan as he drove her as crazy as she made him. Her hands grabbed his hair and her pelvis bucked and trembled as her orgasm hit. His name carried on her scream.

"Easy sweetheart. I got you." He wrapped her legs around his waist, eased one hand into the drawer, pulled out a foil packet, and tore it open with his teeth.

Holding on by a fucking thread, he settled back between Jen's legs. "You okay with this?"

"I'd say so. I want you inside me."

Storm slid inside her and stroked her insides slowly, making sure she was ready for his size. Any which way you looked at it, he was six foot six, and big all over.

Their gazes locked and tiny dots swirled in his vision. Jen was killing him. Energy pulsed from the base of his spine and out the top of his fucking head and he lost it, driving into her like a maniac, every thrust stronger than the last.

"Oh God. I'm co...co...coming."

Jenna's back arched. Her mouth opened in a silent scream. His heart thundered in his chest as he followed her over the edge. Chin resting on the top of her head, he struggled for breath. Who knew how long it took before he rolled to the side and folded her in his arms? *I will never let you go.*

J enna frowned. The idea of spending the day sans undies she could cope with, especially if it meant staying in bed with the gorgeous man lying next to her.

One arm across her chest, his leg pinning her lower body to the mattress, she was quite happy to count the dots on the ceiling. Last night had been... amazing, spectacular? All the above and more. No words could describe what they had shared, and she wanted to do it all over again.

But daydreaming wasn't going to magic a clean pair of knickers. Storm may have no problem with bare skin next to his jeans, but she preferred less exposure.

"Time to move." She gripped Storm's wrist, lifted his fingers from her navel, and emptied a giggle into the sleepy morning.

"Never." His deep growl reverberated against her neck and rumbled its way to her heart. Warm. At home.

"Don't make me make you, Mister. I have no clean underwear."

"I can't see the problem." One eye open, Storm peered at her.

Jenna's fist hovered too long over Storm's nose. She had bated the bear. He flipped onto his stomach, pinned her to the bed, and hummed against the corner of her mouth.

"Commando is a Sentinel uniform standard, but I like my knickers."

"How do you know that?" His head tilted to the side.

"What," she teased.

"That my teammates don't..."

"Wear underwear? Oh, baby, yours isn't the only alpha arse I've seen in my clinic."

Storm slipped his knee between her thighs, stretched one lazy arm over the edge of the bed and skewered her thong on the end of his pinkie.

"I'm not sure this is essential civilian clothing." He grinned and twirled the scrap of silk above his head. "Doesn't seem big enough to miss."

"Hilarious. Now, give it to me." Jenna made a grab for her underwear, well aware of how precariously her right breast dangled beneath his lips.

"Told you, babe. Whatever you need." He bit her nipple, making her yelp.

Jenna's fingers dug into the top of his shoulders. "You are impossible."

"Nope. You figured me out."

His mouth moved slowly, his tongue licking underneath her breasts. Writhing under his attention, she squirmed with pleasure, and an urge to get to the bathroom and out the door to work. "Off." Jenna shoved Storm's head from her body before he reached the point of no return and rolled off the bed.

One arm flung across closed eyes, he flipped to his back. She grinned at the cute tent halfway along the sheets. He groaned. Oh, yeah—spectacularly aroused. And she had done that to him. That kind of girl power came with a sense of triumph that made her girlie bits tingle. "To hell with the washing," she said and leaped on top of him.

"Oomph! Good decision. Fuck your knickers."

"Knickers? You'll be adding blimey to your vocabulary next."

Chapter Thirty-One

"Thank you, Linda. You are a lifesaver. Having the supplies here tonight has saved me loads of time tomorrow morning." Jenna stopped there. No one wanted to hear her whine about how busy she was. They all were.

Honestly, when Snake offered to loan her medical provisions from Sentinel's store, until the Hub's order arrived, she hadn't expected Linda to bring them to the clinic.

"I almost refused. Delivery chick is another Sentinel expectation that isn't in my job description." Linda rolled her eyes at the peeling paint hanging from the ceiling. "Lucky you are on my way home."

"I appreciate it. Coffee and a Danish on me for the rest of the week," she said, hoping sugary pastries might sweeten Linda's personality.

"No need. I'll settle for you sharing how you wrap the boss around your pinkie."

The less than subtle hint that she was in some way special made her uncomfortable. With no smart comeback coming to mind, Jenna bit the inside of her cheek and shrugged.

"I can't help you put stuff away. Gotta go. My cat needs feeding."

"Right. No problem. Enjoy your evening." Jenna went with her and shut the metal door behind her. Linda was a lot like her mother. Nothing too much trouble or inconvenient, unless it involved doing you a favor.

"Argh." Jenna scrubbed the back of her neck. "Tea. I need tea." Her cry echoed through the empty, creepy-quiet clinic. Being the last to leave gave her the creeps, to be avoided most days. Today, the others were long gone. The boxes could wait another ten minutes. The small kitchen was on the way, so why not stop by the small kitchen and turn on the kettle?

Her coworkers teased her when she bought it, complete with a whistle. They drank from the jug of filtered coffee. Brown at the beginning of the day and a muddy black by the end. Grinning at her own stubborn refusal to use the piped in hot water, she flipped the kettle's switch.

Only Sam understood how the ritual of brewing a nice, strong cuppa re-set her world, and helped her think. Filling the kettle. Listening to the water rumble and hiss while she flipped a tea bag into her favorite cup and waited for it to boil.

Drops of condensation trickled down the cold wall, dragging her thoughts along with them. Storm had woken her twice last night. Both times, finding pleasure spots on her body she didn't know existed. The kettle whistled.

Breathing in the earthy aroma of water splashing onto tea leaves, she added milk and a large spoonful of sugar. Hopefully, the brew would lift her mood and stop her from falling asleep on her feet.

Storm had rung earlier to apologize for sending Dexter to pick her up tonight. Poor guy was outside, sitting in his car, waiting to take her home. Didn't seem fair to keep him hanging around too long so she hurried to the window by her desk, but even with her nose against the pane, her hand shielding the overhead light's reflection, she couldn't see anything in the alley at this time of night.

Her ears pricked to attention at the shuffling coming from over by the boxes. One of the others said they'd seen evidence of a mouse. Jenna doubted it. The place was spotless, but the building was old and even Tom and Jerry felt the cold. She would rather step into the eye of a hurricane than face a tiny rodent. If she ignored it and drank her tea, maybe it would leave.

Wrapping her icy fingers around her warm cup, she blew on the rising steam and picked up the file she'd been reading when Linda arrived. Maisy Stone, the woman she treated earlier in the week.

Shy, twenty-five years old, pregnant with her sixth child. Little more than a kid when her parents joined a weird cult and married her off to the perfect partner. A man, twice her age, who refused to keep his dick in his pants long enough for Maisy to recover between pregnancies.

Jenna shook her head. Her role was to ensure mum, her children, including her unborn baby, stayed healthy, not to judge. Some days, she did better than others.

Unfortunately, during Maisy's last pregnancy, gestational diabetes resulted in ongoing health concerns. Jenna scribbled a reminder note for extra pre-natal tests at her next appointment and closed the file.

Before she left, she should call Tom, except Dexter may have a cat to feed, too. Every time she spoke with her son, Jenna hated herself for wishing he'd ask to come home.

No, having far too much fun. Besides, he was where he needed to be, safe with people who cared for him like family. He loved Sam's dogs. Helping her in the kennels gave him space to grieve for Tina without an over-protective mother, in fix-it mode, breathing down his neck.

Besides, enjoying another night of getting to know Storm better certainly appealed. As he might not get home until late, she had time to make dinner. Steak and salad. Ice cream in the freezer for dessert.

She glared at the boxes. Unpacking them could wait until the morning. That should give any mouse enough time to have a chew on the cardboard corner and fall asleep in his hole.

Jenna shut down the computer for the night, made a mental note to order a couple of traps, and took her bag from the bottom drawer of her desk. Turning off the lights as she walked, she headed for the exit.

Light from the street leaking through the window played tricks with her eyes. The building supervisor fumigated every six weeks, but, at night, the cockroach brigade loved to come out and play.

Ugh. Jenna braced for the crackle and squish of one of them under her shoe. She promised Sam if the monsters learned to fly, she would be on the next plane out of Manhattan.

On the way out, she needed to make a quick detour to the ladies' room. Too much tea. In the semi-darkness, she rinsed her hands. Water went everywhere, where a sudden crash of metal made her jump. She turned off the tap and froze. That had to be one giant mouse.

Calm down Jenna. One of her coworkers must have forgot something. Glass smashed, and a man cursed. Immediately, her eyes swung to the small window three quarters of the way up the wall and the door. Too small to make it out of the window, she cracked open the door and squinted at the dimly lit corridor. Across from her, a figure limped between the row of chairs in the waiting area.

At the sight of the man wearing a ski mask and holding a gun, her mind detoured to late night tv thrillers, switchblades, and serial killers. A scream bubbled under the surface as she eased the door shut.

The clinic's no locks policy had to be one of the dumbest. An agenda item for the monthly board meeting. Junkies looking for their next fix burgled the Hub every couple of months, and trashed the place when they realized no narcotics or cash were kept on site. Could have read the sign on the door and saved everyone the hassle.

Panic trembled through the hairs on the back of her neck. Had Hassan found her? She swiped her clammy hands down her coat and went for the phone in her pocket. *The phone you left on the shelf above the sink.*

Her breath caught. She couldn't be sure, but judging by the sound of his footsteps, he'd left the waiting area and headed away from the bathroom. She had to move now. Snatching her phone from the shelf, she slipped into the corridor and made it halfway to the door before he came out of the kitchen. *Damn.* Jenna ducked behind a gurney.

"Come out. I know you're there," he yelled.

Like hell. She crouched closer to the overhanging sheet. It smelled of floral washing powder mixed with enough Lysol to make her sneeze. Taking a deep breath, she pulled her knees to her chest and stared at the phone vibrating in her hand.

Storm: *You on your way home?*

Jenna: *No. At the clinic. There's a man.*

Storm: *What man?*

Jenna: *MAN WITH A GUN.* She sighed.

Storm: *Are you in your office?*

Jenna: *No.* Why did it matter?

Storm: *Find the nearest room and lock the door. I'm on my way.*

Her heart stopped when the screen went blank. But Storm would come. All she had to do was survive. Jenna pushed her back against the wall, used her legs to stand, and bolted across the corridor into one of the treatment rooms.

Dark as hell. She looked around for something to use as a weapon. The cheap stapler would fall apart on impact. The wicker rubbish basket had trouble staying upright on its own. A book? *Grey's Anatomy*. A swift slam against his head with the tome and he'd be out cold.

Keeping one foot wedged against the door, she grasped it from the shelf with both hands. "Hell!" Balance off, the potential weapon fell on the floor. Thinking her foot made an effective door stop proved she'd lost her mind. Who could blame her? The man burst into the room. His fat fingers dug into her arm and he threw her against the floor.

Jenna screamed. Ignoring the tiny dots swimming in front of her. Before she scrambled to her knees, his body slammed her to the ground. He smelled of alcohol and sweat.

"Where do you think you're going?" His fingers curled around her throat.

Fighting for air, she lashed out and dug her nails into his cheeks.

"Bitch!" His black eyes gleamed with fury.

With a roar, he released her, allowing her to claim a breath, before his fist collided with her cheek. He sneered and raised his hand for a second punch. *Oh no.* Jenna dodged right, and his hand smashed into the solid surface beside her ear.

Taking advantage of precious seconds, while he growled like a grizzly with a thorn in his paw, she half crawled to the back exit. But her throbbing head and blurry vision made her slow, and he yanked on her ankle.

"Come here."

"Say, please, arsehole," she slurred, and gripped the door handle above her head. Her knuckles turned whiter than icing on a Christmas cake as she held on, praying that if Storm was on his way, he'd get here fast.

Enraged, scared to bloody death, Jenna aimed her free foot at the intruder's crotch. When it failed to make contact, she drove her heel into his shin.

"Jen." Storm's voice bellowed from the front of the empty building.

About time, lover. Head spinning, her fingers numb, Jen gnashed her teeth like a rabid dog ready to bite off her attacker's balls and lashed out with her foot again.

"Get off her, mother fucker."

Eyes teeming with thunderous rage, Storm charged straight for them.

Chapter Thirty-Two

S torm ran to his Jeep. The beat of heart thumping every bone in his body. Fear threatened to paralyze him as he started the engine and swung the steering wheel into action.

Struggling to get oxygen past his throat and into his belly, every worst-case scenario bombarded him. The beat of the windshield wipers echoed his terror as he gunned the seven-and-a-half-minute drive to the Hub, knowing it took less than a second to die.

And where the fuck was Dex? Why Snake didn't fire him after the rookie allowed a teenager to give him the slip beggared belief.

God help his ass if he'd screwed up a second time. Keeping one hand on the wheel, he stabbed his speed dial with his index finger. "Pick up, dammit." *Hell. Pull yourself together.* One kiss had changed his entire life. Impossible, insane. True.

The light turned red. *No way.* He slammed his foot on the accelerator and sped straight through. Several more blocks zoomed past before he swerved in beside a van a couple of vehicles along from Dex's SUV.

Storm lunged onto the sidewalk, slowed his breathing, and grabbed his Glock from the holster on the passenger seat. Staying low, nice and slow, he snuck behind the van, reached Dex's ride and wrenched open the door. His gut knew what he'd find.

Sentinel's latest recruit slumped over the steering wheel, surprisingly alive. Although, given the amount of blood pooling around him, not for long. "Hang in there, man." Storm alerted 911 and kept moving.

Two hands wrapped around his weapon, he stopped at the Hub's metal entry, and inched it open with the toe of his boot. Total darkness, except for the green light flickering above the rear exit, and Jenna hanging off the back door handle like a fish on a hook.

A man twice her size fought to break her grip while she lashed out with her feet. Terror ripped through his chest. Swear to God, this woman was gonna kill him.

Jenna spotted him. No, she mouthed, shaking her head, the color leeching from her face. He ignored her. Doc had no idea what he was capable of, what he would do to protect her.

"Hey," Storm roared. Fuckhead turned. Blood streamed from his nose. At some point, Jen had made contact, and his chest swelled with pride for his warrior.

Taking advantage of the guy's surprise, Storm charged, crashed two-hundred-and-forty pounds of solid muscle into the fucker and brought him both to the ground.

With one knee planted on numb nuts sternum, he hauled his upper body off the floor. "Now I have your attention. Listen up." A shower of spit his the asshole's nose as Storm dragged him to within an inch of his face. "I'm going to tear your heart out and make you eat it."

Jenna gasped, but he kept his gaze riveted to the man pinned under his knee and pushed his Glock into the center of his forehead.

"You're dead," the idiot snarled and tried to raise his weapon.

Storm bashed his wrist with his elbow. The gun flew in Jen's direction. If he didn't need answers, he'd keep his promise and end this fucker.

Jen scrambled for the weapon and pointed it at shit for brains. *That's my woman.* "You okay?" Her hands shook and her eyes were popping out of their sockets. Dumb question, but he had to hear her voice. "Answer me. Are you hurt?"

The man roared. With a smirk, Storm blocked his attempt at a headbutt with a blow to his broken nose. When he yelped, he punched him again. And another for luck. "See this, fucker?" He pressed his Glock deeper into the man's skull. "Quit moving, or pinkie swear, dipshit, I'll make ground beef of your brain."

"Fuck you."

"Fuck me?" This guy was starting to piss him off. Storm released the safety. Jenna winced. "Doc. Put down that gun and tell me you're okay."

"Yes. Bit dizzy." Her head shook in the negative.

Storm shit sure recognized shock. Jen needed a medic. Right fucking now. Where the hell was the calvary?

"On your feet, asshole." Storm gripped the dirt bag's shirt, hauled him upright, and threw him against the opposite wall. "Who sent you?"

"You know, mother fucker."

He had a damn good idea. Jenna gnawed her bottom lip, tears streaming down her face. "Stay here." Why make her watch him beat a confirmation out of douchebag?

Storm lugged the groveling excuse for a human out back. The stench of piss blended with the tang of blood pouring from his face.

Seconds later, a single shot rang out, and his captive went limp, cheating him out of the satisfaction of beating the fucker to death. Storm released the weight hanging off his fingers, ducked behind the garbage dumpster, and panned his weapon in a slow arc. Whoever fired guessed he'd show sooner or later, and he fucking obliged.

Empty soda cans tossed by the wind, and stray pieces of cardboard hit his boot. Other than that, nothing so much as blinked. No sign of the shooter. His gaze shifted to the back door. Jen better not be curious.

Sirens wailed in the distance. Arriving in less than two was his guess. Looking for any clue to the man's identity, he rifled through his pockets. Zip ID. But like he said, Storm knew who sent him.

He wiped his hands on the guy's jacket and stepped back inside, his skull pounding with adrenaline, fear, and fury. Head bowed, Jenna sat on one of the waiting room chairs, her delicate fingers prodding a nasty cut above her eyebrow.

He had sworn to protect her and failed again. Leaving her with Dexter when his gut warned him it was a mistake to entrust her safety to anyone but him. The second he kneeled beside her Jen screamed.

"Get off m. Leave me alone."

Storm caught the fists pounding his face and neck and cradled them against his sternum. "Hey. It's me. He's gone."

"Dead?"

He nodded.

"Good." Air whooshed from her lungs.

Raise a fist and holler a goddam cheer? Kiss every inch of the woman. Damn if he knew which to do first. "You think you can stand?"

"Yes. Where's Dexter?"

"Outside."

"What? Why didn't he help? Are there more?"

Storm kissed her cheek. "We'll talk about it later, after the medics check you out. Okay?"

"I'm fine, Storm." A wry smile curled her lips.

"Yeah, yeah, Doc. Humor me. Let's hear it for an impartial opinion. On three." With one arm around her waist, the other holding her hand, he took most of her weight and helped her to her feet.

Looking at the deep lines etched into her forehead, she was in a lot more pain than she let on. He bit the inside of his cheek and cursed the shooter. Mother fucker denied him the pleasure of killing the animal who hurt her. "Forgive me, Jen. I should have been here."

"You're here, now. That's what matters." The tips of her fingers brushed his lips.

"Jen?" Her eyes rolled to the back of her head, and she went limp in his arms.

Fuck. Every atom of oxygen left the room. "Talk to me, sweetheart. Jen. Talk to me." He yelled as he sat and cradled her in his lap. Her eyelids flickered. "That's it. I'm right here. Talk to me," he repeated and added a slight shake.

"Whoa. That was weird."

She shuffled on his lap and tried to stand. "Take it easy. You passed out on me."

"Rubbish," she said, and grabbed his hand.

When she started to shake, and each breath turned into a sob, his heart broke. Out front, the metal door crashed open. Two cops, their weapons moving ahead of them, shielded a medic walking behind them.

"Over here." Storm kept his arms locked around Jenna. "Intruder out back. Broke in and attacked the doc, here. He's dead." Storm kept his voice even. Didn't want to spook New York's finest, plus he couldn't let go of her if he tried.

Sure enough, one cop swept his free arm behind him and signaled for the medic to quit moving while the other panned his semi-automatic in their direction. "Not me." Storm shrugged.

Sitrep delivered, he brushed his lips over Jen's head.

"Or me." Jen sniffed and buried her cheek deeper into his chest.

Chapter Thirty-Three

Only Storm could make an offer sound like an order. The attack had caught up with her, shimmering through her body and making her legs tremble. But the big girl inside couldn't let him carry her to his car. Some things she had to do alone, if only to prove to the child inside she wasn't helpless.

Panic hitched a ride on her breath. How difficult would it be to fall into the warmth and strength of his arms? Allow him to lift her free from clear and very present danger. Easy.

Doctor Jenna Fletcher may have trouble putting one foot in front of the other, but Jen, the woman she was learning how to be, had no problem.

"If you won't let me carry you. At least let me help you walk in a straight line," Storm growled.

He strode beside her with his usual confidence and no effort swagger, his large palm cupping her bony elbow. No matter how loudly she protested, Storm didn't know how not to care, not to recognize a soul in trouble. And she was, on every level, with no clue which way to turn. "I'm fine. Walking will do me good. Clear my head."

"No. Fine means you dump the bullcrap and let me help you."

"No," the hoarse echo was pathetic. All she could manage as she swayed into the solid mass of overt masculinity. For a split second, she swayed into the solid mass of overt masculinity, trying to catch her breath, before Storm's arm clamped around her waist. She inhaled his musky scent and felt loved.

A smug grin brought the crinkle lines to the side of his gray eyes, and she did her damndest to stay mad at him. Eighty percent of her wanted to run from the man who saved her life.

"You could have a concussion. You should get checked out," he said softly.

"Stop fussing," she snapped and nodded at his car.

"At least check in with the medic."

"And what am I, chopped liver?"

This time, when Storm grinned, she joined him. Screeching in the street wasn't her style.

"Okay, sweetheart, but just because I'm ex-military, doesn't mean I know every gun in the arsenal."

"Right. Okay, then," she said, realizing her hands were sweaty and the pain in her head made her teeth go on edge.

Storm cupped her cheeks and kissed her. Not one of his hotter than hell lip locks—a graze. Her heart skipped a beat. Their usual sizzling connection felt broken. But when he took her hand and brushed his thumb across her wrist, she took comfort in the fact electricity still shot through her body whenever they touched.

"Come on. Let's get you home."

His voice, huskier than usual, sent shivers rushing along her spine. In the past few days, everything had changed. The world had turned upside down, and it wasn't because of her aching head.

Storm opened the door of his Jeep, lifted her onto her seat, and clicked her seatbelt closed. As his eyes never left her face, she expected, half-hoped, he'd palm the back of her neck and draw her to him for a kiss. Never happened. He hovered for a split second, then ducked around the front to the driver's side.

When he didn't start the car, she assumed the growing tension between them had everything to do with coming down from the hyper zone. They both deserved a minute to pull themselves together, so when Storm's hand stretched across the console and gently squeezed her knee, she let go of the breath she didn't realize she'd been holding.

"Before Dex arrived, did you notice anyone hanging around the clinic? Someone who shouldn't be there?"

Jenna shook her head. "No. I only went outside once, to drop the rubbish in the bin. When he arrived, he texted, and I remember thinking it was too damn cold to sit in his SUV, and I should fetch him. Her bottom lip trembled. "But we were busy, and I forgot. Maybe if..."

"Don't do that. His choice. If he wanted in, he didn't need an invitation."

"Now I think about it, there was this one guy. Smoking. Probably from the projects across the street. They often hang out behind the bins next door. He waved, and I went inside, but he was nothing like the man who... Please. Can we go home? I want to see Tom, and..." Jenna stared at the blood spots on her shirt. "And I need a shower." Before Storm could do the honors, she sniffed and swiped the tear from her cheek.

"Sure thing."

A chill skittered across the top of her shoulders. Dex's SUV was still parked in the same spot, a gurney and a paramedic working on someone inside, but she didn't have the strength to ask questions.

***

It had been a few hours since Storm had been near her. At first, she thought he'd left her alone to shower, because she bit his head off when he tried to help her undress. A decision it didn't take her long to regret as soon as she bent over to pull off her socks.

Lying in bed, no matter which way she shuffled, she couldn't get comfortable. Every bone in her body ached. On the next exhale, she hauled her backside into a sitting position, and reached for the packet of peas Storm had brought her earlier to calm the bruise on her thigh.

"Oh yeah." The tips of her fingers tapped the bruise forming under her eye and blossoming over her cheekbone. The hot shower helped, but her vision was still blurry.

The knock on the door made her jump. Clutching the pillow, she held her breath.

"It's only me," Storm said, easing the door open and poking his head inside.

Despite the bruises, Jenna wished he'd step closer and give her a hug. "Why are you knocking?" It wasn't as though he hadn't seen her, had her, multiple times over, in his bed.

"Wasn't sure if you were asleep. Didn't want to wake you."

So why knock now? His answer made no sense. "Come to bed." She patted the mattress. When he didn't move, rejection sank low in her belly. "Storm?"

The air between them grew thicker. She wondered what she'd done wrong.

"I need to catch up on a few things. You want anything? Tylenol?"

Bloody hell. Damn it, I need you. Her fists hit the sheet, tugging it beneath her bare breasts, and there was no mistaking the spark in his eyes before it died. "Nothing. Thanks."

"Sleep. I'll check in on you in a couple of hours," he said. His firm bicep flexed as he grabbed the edge of the door.

"It's late. Come to bed." Something was bothering him, but she wouldn't beg.

"Like I said. Stuff to do. Text me if you need anything." He turned sideways and slipped behind the door.

Tears pricked her eyeballs. Too tired to follow, insist he spit it out so she could sleep. When the door flew open again, she hadn't moved an inch. Storm towered over the bed, and whatever bothered him still lurked in the smoky shadows of his eyes. "Forget something?"

His grunt could mean many things, but she reached for him, her heart pounding in her chest as he sank one knee onto the mattress beside her hip. The tip of his nose brushed the side of her neck.

Jenna gasped and grabbed his shirt, clinging to him as he kissed her deeply, giving back everything she gave and more.

When he finally broke the kiss, she couldn't breathe. Her emotions in hyperdrive swirled in her head, taking potshots at her heart. Their breaths turned to gasps, and she was on fire. Her fingers caressed his face, the day-old shadow rough under her fingers. She wanted him deep inside her, stroking away the madness.

Their eyes met, and before she could stop him, Storm rolled onto his feet.

"Sorry. That should never have happened," he mumbled.

Her head flopped against the pillow. *What the bloody hell? This is crazy.* No way. They were going to have this out now. But not while she was naked. Careful not to shift her head too far in any direction, she pulled on a pair of sleep shorts and a silk camisole. Too angry to find shoes, she opted for bare feet and headed downstairs.

Voices rumbled in Storm's office. Good. If Snake or Hawke were on the other end of the line, she deserved to hear what they said. Breathing deeply, she braced her hands on the wall for support and made her shaky way to him.

"Please don't cry. I know it's tough, but you can do this," Storm said, his voice oozing with understanding.

A person spoke in hushed tones when they didn't want anyone to interrupt their conversation. The bells clanging in her head had nothing to do with her injury.

"I'll come see you soon, and we will work things out. Please try. For me."

Through the crack in the door, Jenna watched him thump his fist on the counter and silently curse. She'd bet her next pay packet, whoever was on the phone had nothing to do with Sentinel or her.

As soon as her heartbeats stopped colliding with each other, she should go and make a strong cuppa before he saw her. God knows she needed it.

"Jen? What are you doing there?"

Nothing new. She hadn't heard him move. Jenna pointed at the phone in the hand hanging by Storm's side. "Who was that?"

"No one."

"Liar." The room turned into a merry-go-round gone wild. Terrified she'd spew, Jenna clamped her hand over her mouth.

"Let's get you back to bed."

Sunlight sliced through the slats in the blinds. Jenna pinched the bridge of her nose. Too early for the light to be this bright. She had no strength to argue when Storm swung her into his arms and climbed the stairs.

Chapter Thirty-Four

Leave her alone. He should not be touching Jen, certainly not sporting a major hard on as he carried her upstairs. He had failed to protect her. A man in love didn't choose a team briefing over his woman's safety.

As the youngest in his family, he'd always ran scared, frightened of missing something. Not wanting to be left behind, he drove his older brothers mad, tagging along after them. As a man, he made himself indispensable, insisted on being at the briefing when the boss, Trig, any of his Sentinel team would keep him in the loop.

Fixated on his unbroken track record, front and center at every briefing, he sent Dex to pick her up and ignored any possible consequences. And when were there never any fucking consequences?

If he had busted through those clinic doors and found Jen bleeding out on the damn floor. No way could he survive. Life without the beauty that made his heart tick wasn't worth living.

He lay Jen on the bed, pulled the comforter up to her chin, and sat with his back to her, knowing once Hawke confirmed Hassan's location, the team would bug out for Somalia, and he'd be right there with them. Unwilling to let anyone else look the fucker in the eye and annihilate the threat to Jen and Tom.

At the touch of her fingers on his arm, his gut threw a punch at his throat.

"What is it? I get you wanted me to go to Emergency. I know I look like crap and every time my head shifts, I see bloody stars, but I'll be fine after a night's sleep. Now hug me, for Christ's sake."

He leaned in and cupped Jen's cheek, careful not to press the bruise under her eye.

She grabbed his wrists. "That's it. Closer. Kiss me."

He didn't deserve her. The sooner he got the call and put distance between them, the better.

"Come to bed. I need you."

Jenna pushed the cover aside and hooked her arm around his neck. Offering no resistance, he folded her into his arms and held his breath. Afraid he might hurt her, he floated his hands over the pale, naked skin on her shoulder.

Lying there, face to face, her eyes fixed on his. *Jesus.* Storm never wanted any woman more than her, but she almost died because of him. *Leave.* Instead, his mouth claimed hers. Sucking on her bottom lip, he savored everything he craved.

With a moan, her arms wrapped around his neck, binding him to her. "For your information, sweetheart, you do not look like crap. You are beautiful..." His lungs groped for air.

"Good enough to eat?" she whispered.

His balls tightened. "Always. But you're in pain, and..."

"So are you. Tell me. What's going on in that head of yours?" Jenna laid her forehead against his and ran the tip of her finger along the seam between his lips. "Who was on the phone?" she asked.

He ignored the question. Too fucking long and complicated to answer. "I should have been with you at the clinic. Not left it to Dex to protect you."

"You are joking. My rising storm obliterating everything, anyone in its path."

"Jesus, Jen. I want you." *Liar, liar, pants on fire. You need her more than life's blood.*

"So, what's the problem? I'm tough. Promise. You won't hurt me. Please," she moaned. "No more playing hard to get. Start with telling me your name?"

"Turn over." Not sure he could manage that one face-to-face, he helped Jenna roll onto her side, and molded his front to her back. "Matthias."

"There. That wasn't so bad. I was sure you were going to say, Cyril."

"And..." He nuzzled his nose against her ear, slipped his fingers beneath the waistband of her shorts into the heat between her legs. "What if I had?"

"Mmm. I'd have said. Cyril. Make me come."

Music to his fucking ears. He slid a finger inside her, added a second, then a third. Her ass arched into his pelvis as she rode his hand.

"More." She shuddered.

Hungry for a taste of her, he eased her onto her back and swapped his hand for his mouth. The musky tang of her arousal flooded his senses as she rode his face into oblivion and came hard and fast against his tongue.

"Matt."

Hell. With a single word, she claimed him. Made him want to hear his name fall from her lips every day for the rest of his life. Her Matt. His Jen. "Fuck."

"At last, we're on the same page," she gasped.

Storm reached for a condom from the packet on the bedside table. His hand trembled as he undid his zipper and shoved his pants to his knees. He sheathed his cock and guided it to her entrance. The tingling at the base of his spine destroying any intention of going slow, if he ever had any. "I'm close, sweetheart." Small circles of his breath caressed her neck. Her breath hitched.

"Me too. Don't. Hold. Back." Her voice was firm. In control.

Which was more than he could claim. *Fuck.* He loved this woman. The perfect mix of shy and sure. Honest. Adored how she had no problem asking for what she wanted. Demand what she needed.

Storm vowed. The next time Jen came, she'd scream his name. He dug his fingers into her hips, thrust into her steamy heat, and froze. Not daring to move, in case he spilled too soon.

When her fingernails bit his ass, urging him forward, he lost it, pumping into her until his balls tightened. Pleasure-pain hit max, and he exploded. Poured everything he was, and hoped to be, into her.

No scream, but her guttural groans echoed in every dark space inside, transported him to places he'd never dreamed existed. His heart pounded. Lost in her breath, surrounded by the smell of their lovemaking, he stayed glued to her soft, sweet curves until his phone buzzed in the pocket of his jeans.

Jen half laughed, half groaned, and snuggled against his semi-hard dick.

Snake's name flashed across the screen. *Hell.* "Sorry, sweetheart, I have to take this."

"You're sure?"

Jen's internal muscles squeezed tight, making him work to be free. "Hold that thought. I'll be right back." He kissed her shoulder, rolled off the bed, and with his jeans round his ankles, stumbled to the bathroom and closed the door.

"Boss. What's up? He reached for a face cloth, turned on the tap, and ran it under the warm water.

"Location confirmed. Wheels up—one hour. You good to go?" Snake said.

"Yeah. I'll be there."

"I've called in two of Beta's team's best. They'll stay with Doc, won't leave her side until you return."

"Appreciate it. Thanks." Storm hung up. After he disposed of the condom and cleaned himself off, he returned to Jen, intending to tell her about the phone call she'd overheard earlier, but she looked so damn cute asleep where he had left her. He didn't have the heart to wake her, worship her perfect body before he left, so he scribbled a note and placed it beside her on his pillow.

We found him. It's time to end this and bring Tom home. Then the three of us are going to have a long talk about our future. He smiled. That would give Doc something to think about while he was gone. *P.S. Snake has men outside. Stay safe. Matt.*

Chapter Thirty-Five

Something wasn't right. Her lower back tingled with the cold. Lost in half-sleep, Jenna reached behind her for her human hot water bottle. The gentle hero whose tender touch, and tickle-toe kisses, healed her aches and pains, and made her forget.

Right before Storm charged into the clinic, she wasn't sure she'd leave there alive. Last night, buried in his arms, listening to the solid beat of his heart, she let go of the fight.

Alone in bed, half hidden under the covers, she could admit how much she missed him. Hopefully, this morning, during Sentinel's regular early morning PT session, he'd be in a better mood and tell her who'd called. She hadn't noticed the birds chirping until they whistled questions. *Do you really want to know?*

The team work outs were mandatory. In the field, being in prime shape mentally and physically upped the odds of everyone making it home alive. After a long run and a couple of hours pushing weights, he'd be ravenous, craving food. Over the past month, that often meant them feasting on each other.

A long, lazy stretch completed her psych up for getting out of bed. Her stomach growled as she swung her legs over the side of the bed and the soles of her feet hit the parquet flooring. Bless Storm and his underground heating. She closed her eyes and relished the heat thawing her numb toes.

Breakfast. Pancakes, Storm and Tom's favorite. Maybe he'd satisfy her curiosity and share stories. When she thought about it, other than knowing he'd been married and had a military career, he'd shared little of his life before they met.

Light poured through the bedroom window, and sirens wailed. *Argh.* The city that never slept was wide awake this morning. Forget breakfast. She needed to tidy up the clinic and unpack those boxes.

If she finished before anyone else walked into the disaster, she could reschedule her appointments, come home and catch Storm in the shower, share the soap before she crashed. After all, they may not have much time before Snake had them on a plane flying to heaven knew where.

As tempting as that all sounded, she never took a day off. It wasn't until she went searching for clothes to toss in the laundry that she saw the piece of paper sitting next to her thong on the dresser. *Hilarious, big boy.*

It took a second to tease out the knocking on the front door from the traffic noise, and as she didn't feel up to greeting the world half-naked, she ignored it and checked Storm's closet for a baggy T-shirt.

Damn. His pack was missing. Several empty hangers hung on the rod, the gun safe open, his weapon gone. Last night's insecurities crashed in on her. Shaky—empty. The aftereffects of the adrenaline hype sucked. The chances of his note revealing a neat return date were slim to none. Before she could check, the banging started up again, and judging by the insistent rhythm, they weren't going to stop.

Jenna grabbed her robe from the back of the chair and slipped her feet into her slippers. "Okay, okay, I'm coming", she yelled from the top of the stairs. Taking a deep breath, she punched in the alarm code and dragged the door open.

"Who the hell are you?" asked the woman, doing her best to melt into the brownstone walls.

Wind tugged at her long dark hair, pulling it in all directions. Smudged mascara underneath her enormous brown eyes made her look like an angry racoon. "I'm Jenna. Dr. Fletcher," she added, thinking one of the clinic patients must have found her home address. "What do you want?"

"You must be the slut fucking my husband. You look like shit."

Jenna stiffened and tried not to enter the competition.

"Where is he?"

The woman's high-pitched whine grated as Christine, she presumed, pushed past. "If you're looking for Storm. He's not here." Jenna opened the door wider, praying Storm's ex took the hint.

"You begging for another black eye? I won't ask you again, bitch. Where is he?"

Jen's fingers flew to the tender spot on her cheek. "I told you. You're hus... Storm isn't here. Now, please leave." Jenna swept her hand along the floor, looking like a crazed flight attendant in her flimsy robe.

"I'm not going anywhere until I see him. Storm, baby. It's me," Christine yelled. Her hip collided with the doorknob before she pushed the door open and marched into the living room.

"Fine. But you may have to wait a long time. He's gone, as in out of the country—at work."

A laugh, more a cackle, wracked Christine's tall, clinically underweight body, and that's when her professional instincts kicked in. The woman wasn't well and clearly stressed.

"Work? Ha! No fucking surprise. Welcome to the club, sister." Christine swayed and grabbed hold of a chair.

From bitch to sister in less than five minutes. Jenna leaned against the wall. "Like I said, I'm not sure when Storm will be back."

"Of course you aren't." Christine clicked her fingers. "Disappeared. I'll say this for my man. He sure knows how to work a puff of smoke. I'm off doing spooky stuff, baby. You don't need the details. That's the way it goes. Am I right?" She pouted. "How long have you been fucking my husband?"

Oh, that was it. Jenna took two steps into the middle of Christine's space. "Listen, *sister*. I don't know what you want, and, frankly, I don't care, but I have to get to work, and you have to go. You can leave Matt a note?"

"Matt! Who the fuck is that? No, save it. *I don't care.*"

Christine mimicked Jenna's English accent. Christ, she felt sorry for Storm's ex. This close, it was difficult to miss her clammy skin and trembling hands.

"Storm is mine, bitch, and I need to see him right now."

Here we go again. When Christine leaned sideways and had to take a few steps to stop from falling. Jenna grabbed her arm, steadied her, and gasped at the strong chemical smell on the woman's breath. Dilated pupils. An addict. Jenna softened her voice. "Is there something I can do to help?"

"Storm owes me." In between rapid eye blinks, she licked her lips. "You're lying. He can't be gone. I spoke to him yesterday. He promised to take care of me," she whined.

Last night, she'd asked Storm twice who he had been speaking to, and both times he evaded her question. A tear, crocodile or otherwise, rolled over Christine's cheek.

Jenna shook her head. Not knowing what else to do, she pulled her phone from her pocket and called him. Of course, it went to voice mail. *Damn.* "I've tried his number, there's no answer, and I really must leave. Write your note, and I'll make sure he gets it as soon as I see him. If you come with me to the clinic, I can get you some help."

Her heart shrank to the size of a pea. After promising herself to stay clear of men, she'd trusted Storm. *Stupid, stupid.* He might not be married to Christine, but she was still a major part of his life. She needed to think. See her son.

Lost in thought, with her back turned, didn't realize Christine had left until a gust of wind whistled under the stairs, and the front door banged shut. It was clear the woman needed help. Why didn't she do more to make her stay? Battered inside and out, Jenna sent Storm a text.

Jenna: Need time to think. I'll call you. Jenna.

Chapter Thirty-Six

Where the hell was she? Storm swiped at the kamikaze flies circling his head and reached for his flask. One swill of the lukewarm water was enough before he spat it into the dust. A hundred degrees in the shade. Twitching his fucking pinkie took too much energy.

Unfortunately, his gut ache had nothing to do with the drink or the heat and everything to do with the images bombarding his fucking brain. Main one—Jenna gripping the clinic door, frantically kicking at the guy who dared lay a hand on her.

He wanted to lock her up, hide her from the world where no one looked for the fearless medic who fought with everything in her to stave off her attacker. But the fucker was big, and she was small. If he'd arrived two minutes later? No. He wasn't going there again.

He lay awake watching the rise and fall of her chest, listening to his heat skip a beat every time her breath hitched. The bruises on her face and neck gutted him.

Should never have happened. No better than Dex, he failed to protect her. From the start, Jenna said hooking up with him was a bad idea. He should have listened, tucked his alpha dick back in his boxers, and left her to have a nice life.

Before they boarded the plane, he'd called her, and like a fucking coward, when she didn't answer, he left a message telling her she was right all along. Too bad the boss witnessed his meltdown and ordered him to stay behind, but this was where he belonged. With his brothers, working to take out Hassan and end the threat. Snake put it to him straight. Get his shit together or he or one of his teammates would arrive home feet first.

Trig kicked his boot. "Cheer the fuck up, will ya? My guess, after spending time with your horny ass, Jenna's sleeping, getting ready for makeup sex when she sees you."

His friend nodded once, convinced he had the situation covered. Storm took the point even if he cringed at Trig, slipping the words, sex, and Jenna into the same sentence.

Storm flattened another kamikaze insect, swooping for his mouth. "Man, I swear Hassan trains these flies, using my face as a homing beacon."

"Be thankful they ain't tsetse flies sucking on your ass." Winter lifted his helmet and swept a hand over his damp hair.

Ass? Oh no. Not going there. Thanks to Jen's healing touch, Storm's rear had healed fine, and he shit sure didn't need painful reminders of the fuck up that landed them here. "I hate goddam flies," he raged at the bluer than blue sky.

"Yeah, and Knight hates rain. The two of you make a great couple." Havoc swiped his hand across his mouth, as impressed with the bilge swill in his flask as much as Storm.

"Ain't that the goddam truth," Winter agreed.

Storm chuckled. Sentinel's founder rarely left London HQ to visit, and when he did, it poured as soon as his boot hit the tarmac. Mother-fucking hilarious, watching the mean guy run for cover.

As the temperature continued to climb, the group fell silent and conserved their energy. Hawke's coordinates had them waiting on the outskirts of a Somalian village, an Al Shabaab stronghold. Surrounded by maize, sorghum, and acacia trees, they ran the battle plan and counted the seconds until Hassan showed his hairy chin.

"Third house to the left of the borehole."

Over the comms, Hawke's voice battled with the screeching cicadas.

"Copy that," Snake answered. "Move."

Havoc went first, taking up a position behind an obliging tree. Storm scanned the surrounding hills, looking for Winter. There one minute, AWOL the next. Zip surprise. Snipers got off on that Where's Waldo shit. Fucking déjà vu.

Numbnuts had to know they were coming. Using granddad and the boy as a shield was his first mistake. Targeting the people Storm loved, his last. Hassan deserved every nick and slice of his blade.

"Backend. You in position?" Trig snickered over the comms.

Swear to God. "Copy that," Storm grumbled. Shaking his head, he ducked behind the building opposite their target and eased his pack from his shoulder.

"Got you covered, front, side and..." Winter cleared his throat. "Rear."

"Funny, asshole." Most times on a mission, the old guy saved his breath until he said his favorite words. *Target Down.*

"Shut the fuck up," Havoc rasped.

Best Bud.

"Let's do this and go home. Mia wanted to talk, and I asked her to wait. I'm regretting it." Havoc grunted.

Time to gear up. With zero plans to use it unless he had to, Storm holstered his Glock and sheathed his M3 trench knife in the horizontal hip holster. His preferred bed mate over the Ka-bar. Confident his brothers were doing the same, the scrapes and clicks of weapons engaging as natural to them as breathing, he held out his hands in front of him. Steady as a rock. *Come to daddy.*

"Heads up, eyes in." Hawke said.

Glory, hallelujah for her drones. A truck, the rear end covered in camo canvas, tires crunching the dirt, rolled out of a shed a few doors up from the target's building.

A bunch of men rode in the back, their faces covered, packing enough ammo to make Armageddon look like a picnic. Trig signaled to let them pass.

"Two armed tangos, one at the front, the other at the rear door. Another in the second room to the right. No visible weapon. Most likely, Hassan." Hawke gave the intel on the heat signatures on the bodies inside Hassan's, her voice clear and even.

"How can we be sure it is Hassan?" Havoc asked.

"Good fucking question. Let's find out. Moving." Trig replied.

"Moving." Storm confirmed.

They shifted positions and headed in arrow formation for Hassan's front door. A swift kick from Havoc's combat boot and it collapsed. Storm tossed in a flashbang. *Boom.*

The butt of Havoc's weapon cracked open the sentry's skull, and first blood splashed over Storm's Kevlar vest. Trig pressed forward. Two taps, one to the chest, one to the head, and the wall wore the second sentry.

Bullets ricocheted off the plaster close to Havoc's head. He swiveled, silenced the threat and slid behind Trig, who now stood opposite. One hand raised, the boss halted their assault at the entrance to what they assumed was Hassan's inner sanctum and eyeballed him.

Storm nodded. No need to draw fucking straws. This murdering son-of-a-bitch was his. Inhaling deeply, he palmed the hilt of his M9.

"Incoming. Five-hundred meters." Hawke's voice bled through his headpiece. "Stop playing with the shithead," she drawled.

The sweat on the back of Storm's neck turned cold. "Cover me," he demanded.

Smooth as, the boss' fingers counted down, then, three, two, one, the butt of his weapon splintered the wood. A single shove of Snake's shoulder busted the door off its hinges and cleared his path.

Unarmed, quaking like the mother fucker coward he was, Hassan jumped to his feet and shouted, "Allahu Akbar." *God is great.*

Storm winked. "Must be, asshole. Thank the almighty for me, and keep your hands off those virgins." With zero regret, he collared Hassan with one arm, sliced his throat, and tossed him onto the dirt floor.

Bleeding out too fast, in his opinion, shock glinted in the fucker's black eyes. He leaned over the dying man. "This is for Tina. You piece of shit." With the tip of his thumb, he swiped blood from the edge of his knife and marked Hassan's forehead with a capital T.

Snake's palm landed on Storm's shoulder. "Okay. Job done, my friend. Let's go home."

"About fucking time. Incoming, fifty meters." Hawke warned.

Chapter Thirty-Seven

The fire crackled and popped, glowed with heat that defied any bone in Jenna's body to resist its love. Her phone peered at her from under the patchwork quilt. George raised his head and puffed out a heavy sigh when she nudged it with her finger.

"Okay, boy. I won't answer it." Even if it did ring. Sam insisted she loved torture. Close friends earned their title, nailing your inner demons.

Storm's call and texts began as soon as she left his place and continued all the way to Sam's. In a twisted way, she hated that they'd suddenly stopped when she arrived at the farm. Then Sam told her the team was chasing down Hassan. Now, she'd give her left foot for a glimpse of his name on her screen.

"I'm putting the kettle on. You want tea?" Sam sang from the kitchen.

"Mmm." Jenna stretched her arms over her head and unfurled her legs. "Sure. Let me help." Her fingers itched to take the phone with her, but she settled for a pat and walked away. George lifted his head, but decided he wasn't up for tea. "Look after it for me, boy."

"What's your fancy?" Sam nodded at the neat row of pastel-colored tins on the bench.

Jenna smiled. From *Rock Your Socks* to *Snooze or Booze*, each tin wore a perfectly lined up label. "Heard anything?" She reached for *Make or Break* and one of the cup-for-one teapots on the shelf and popped it beside Sam's.

"I hear plenty. A miracle, considering it's me and the dogs out here alone most of the time. Sam filled the teapots with water.

"You know what I mean." Jenna pulled the milk from the fridge.

"Oh. Any. Thing? As in a large, gorgeously proportioned thing, with one of the best arses ever to wear denim. Second to my husband."

"Argh. I'm going to hit you. Storm? Have you heard?"

"Careful. Those hands are a gift, meant to heal, not hurt."

"Sam." Jenna warned.

"Okay. No. You know how it is." Her voice turned serious. "Comms are dark until they walk up that long path to the front door."

Jenna turned the teapot three times clockwise for good luck, just like her gran had taught her.

Sam stilled her hand before she went for a fourth turn of the pot. "When are you going to tell me what happened? Don't get me wrong, I love having you here, but why did you leave Storm's? Your work at the Hub?"

Jenna shrugged. "No reason. Time to move on, and the Hub can do without me for a few days. What's so odd about wanting to see my son? And you."

"Better tell her, mum. She's never going to stop nagging until you do."

Hanging out with Storm, her son had picked up his light foot habits. "Tom."

"Mum."

He had his dad's eyes, and they were gawking at her as if she'd sprung two heads. "Okay, okay. After Storm left, Christine showed up demanding I magic her husband out of thin air. I didn't feel like getting involved in their domestic, so I left. Simple." Angry at herself for spiraling into the dark place she hated, she raised her chin and clenched her jaw. "And before either of you says anything. I get he has a piece of paper confirming they're..." She air quoted her next word. "Divorced, but it seems they are still very much co-dependent."

Tom rolled his eyes. "So, are you and Storm a couple or not?" he asked, taking a bite from his apple.

Sam nudged Tom's elbow. "About time, right, mate?"

"Don't you dare." Jenna warned. "Tom, I'm not sure what you mean by a couple." Her face flushed. The kid's eyes somersaulted in their sockets. "Look. It's no big deal. We're exploring our options."

"Wow, that sounds like a board meeting rather than a fu…"

"Stop!" Channeling Mary Poppins, for Christ's sake, she stamped her foot.

"Okay, okay." Sam's lips curled into a teasing smile.

"Whatever." Tom flashed a cocky grin, as if he already had his answer.

Desperate for a little breathing space, she opened the refrigerator door and hid behind it. "What does everyone want for dinner? I'll cook." Nose in the air, George padded into the kitchen. "Yes, you, too, boy."

"Nothing for me. I ate. I'm going to check on the pups. It's cold. Okay if I sleep in the barn tonight, Sam, in case they need me?" Tom asked.

"Sure. There are extra blankets in the box by the door. Stay warm."

"'Night, mum. Love you." Tom kissed her cheek and left.

One down. Jenna sipped her tea and sauntered over to the couch. "Will he be okay out there?" she asked, flopping onto the soft leather. Sam collapsed beside her, splashing a few drops of *Rock Your Socks* on her jeans. Jen reached for a tissue and dabbed them dry.

"Sure. Snake patched up the roof and mum won't let her pups stray far from their bed in the hay."

"I am an idiot." Jen sighed.

"Got that right." Sam clicked her fingers and called George to come and sit at her feet. "He's growing up fast."

"No. Tom's fine, but just when I think I've pushed through my hangups after Baxter, Christine comes along and stirs up all my insecurities. Not proud of myself, but I ran. I'm rooting for my brain to catch up with my heart and tell me to stop. Make sense?"

"Fuck, no. Listen, lady. I've known Storm for a while now, and he is nothing like Baxter. Bedding two at a time, not his style. As for physically hurting a woman? He'd die first. I admit he has a complicated relationship with Christine. The marriage is over, but the protector gene runs deep in all the Sentinel men. Ex or not, he will never abandon her."

Jenna laid her head on her friend's shoulder. Trust Sam to tell her straight. Her throat tightened. "I didn't answer his calls or texts."

"Sister. You are in big trouble." Sam chuckled. "It'll be okay. When he gets back, talk to him. Now, up, on your feet and quit the pity party. You promised me dinner. Your son may have eaten, but I'm craving a blue steak with all the trimmings."

At the sound of another of his trigger words, George barked twice. "Wait, a minute. Craving? You are not?"

"Pregnant. God, no." Sam gave her a shove. "Although the way we go at it." She smiled. "I'd say it's inevitable. Sooner rather than later."

Jenna grabbed her friend's cup. "Fine. Light up that bar-b-que gizmo, and let's have at it. Do you want chips with your steak, and I don't mean those matchstick fries, or a salad?" Jenna winked.

"Greens are for wimps. Said my granddad. The man with the largest garden allotment in North London. Fat chips drowning in cheese. Gimme."

George at heels, and a swipe at the infuriating tear in the corner of her eye, she went on the hunt for potatoes. Made it as far as the vegetable drawer before gunshots sent a shiver rattling down her spine. *Tom.*

Her gaze swung to the front door as her shin collided with the edge of the kitchen island. Ignoring the pain, she stumbled outside. Stinging rain smacked her face and caught her breath.

"*Pas Auf.*" Sam yelled at George.

The military trained K9 responded to her command to guard and stood in front of her. "Out of my way, boy." The dog didn't move. Jenna peered through the deluge toward the barn. There was a white van, parked near the gate at the bottom of the first paddock. Memories of the night of the fire in England, when Tom almost died, ripped across her vision. *Not again.* "Have to get to Tom."

"Okay, wait." Sam grabbed her coat from behind the door and hooked her fingers under George's collar. "Stay behind me. George, *Aus.*"

Together, they headed into the wind. Halfway to the barn, George froze, bared his teeth and growled at the man getting out of the van. A gun in his hand.

"Run." Sam shoved her sideways.

If he'd heard the shots, her son would hide. Jenna banked on it and turned back to Sam as Tom emerged from the barn. "No. Go back," she yelled. George kept barking. The world moved at a terrifying pace. Her feet shuffled in some kind of crazy dance as she tried to work out which way to turn.

Another shot echoed in the night. Sam spun in a half circle and fell on the ground. George howled. Jen dropped to her knees beside her and pleaded with Tom to find cover.

Blood oozed from Sam's right arm. Jen threw the left one over her shoulder and heaved her to her feet.

"*Ruhig*. Quiet, boy." Sam rasped.

Jenna almost died when Tom broke cover and ran to help get Sam inside the house. "Lock the door. Set the code."

"What the fuck?" Sam slurred.

"Over here." Jenna stumbled to the couch and lowered Sam as gently as she could onto the cushions. "Tom, stay away from the window and get behind that chair." She lifted her chin at Snake's favorite by the fire.

Placing her arm under Sam's legs, she lifted them onto the couch. "Has he gone?" she asked, as if Sam had the answer. She lowered the zipper on Sam's coat. "Let me take a look."

"I'm fine. Just a scratch." Sam moaned.

"Be quiet and stay still," she ordered. A single bark from George and his mistress knew she was outnumbered.

Sam groaned and laid her head against the couch.

"And don't you dare pass out on me. I can't do this alone." Jenna checked Sam's arm. No major damage, but there was a lot of blood. "You need stitches. A hospital." She looked around for something to bind the injured arm. *Bless untidy teenagers.* "Tom, slowly reach for your T-shirt. It's on Snake's seat and throw it along the floor to me."

Before he could do as she asked, George crawled on his haunches, snagged the T-shirt from the chair and brought it to her. "Thanks, boy." Jenna kept one eye on the door and ripped the T-shirt into strips.

Once she'd secured the bandage high and tight on Sam's arm, she reached under the quilt for her phone. "Damn. No reception." Tom stared at her, his face pale, eyes the size of a harvest moon.

"Okay. The bleeding has stopped, and seeing as that son of a bitch hasn't burst through the door, I'm going for help."

"No. Too dangerous," Sam groaned.

All heads turned to the sound of the door rattling on its hinges. "It's the wind," she said, trying hard not to sound like she was asking a question. "Tom. As soon as I leave, keep trying to call the cops."

"No. Don't go," Tom said, his voice scratchy.

"Shh. It's okay. George will stay with you." The dog pressed his nose into her hand. "The neighbor across the paddock can drive for help and I'll come right back." She didn't want to risk starting Sam's truck. Better the man outside believed all three of them were trapped inside the house.

Crouching low, Jenna crawled over to her son and gave him a quick hug. "I love you. You got this. Watch, Sam."

"Me, too. Come back quick."

Tom's faint smile broke her heart.

Chapter Thirty-Eight

Like a kid eager to start his vacation, Storm leaned forward as if sheer willpower could force Snake's pickup to move faster. *How much longer?* In truth, Snake had made damn good time. They'd dropped off Havoc and Trig in the city, Winter in Brooklyn, before stopping by his to pick up a change of clothes. Snake's palm landed in the middle of his chest.

"Relax, friend. Sit back and spare my fucking windshield from your head butts. We will be there within the hour."

With a grunt, his head skirting the roof, Storm shuffled backward. Over the last five miles, the rain had turned to sleet, making the road too treacherous to travel at any great speed no matter how much he wanted to lay eyes on Jen.

He never expected what the guys had with their women to happen to him, but she was it. And after he squashed whatever bee crawled under her bonnet, he intended making it official. If she'd have him.

For the thousandth time since he'd opened his front door and found her gone, his stomach flipped. Sure, she was pissed at him for keeping quiet, not telling her Christine had called that night, but there was more. If she'd just answer one of his calls, he'd beg for a chance to explain.

Outside his window, the world rushed by. Not that he could see a goddam thing except for Jen's face rising like a phantom every couple of yards.

"You sure turning up on my doorstep is your best plan?" Snake rubbed his sleeve over the windshield.

"Yep." Storm raised an eyebrow, surprised he asked. "She's ignoring my calls. This is something I gotta do face-to-face." *Kiss some sense into her.* He kept that key piece of intel to himself as they flew past another exit.

A truck pulled alongside them, its wheels spraying slush against the window. He slipped his phone out of his pocket to send Sam a text, letting her know they were almost there. When he called from the airport, she confirmed Jen and Tom were at the farm. It helped, knowing she was safe.

Hawke's name flashed on his screen. "Shouldn't you be sleeping?" Remembering the last time he'd called and caught her between the sheets, a smile dragged on the corners of his mouth.

"I should, but... You sitting down, friend?"

Her tone turned his blood cold. Instinctively, Storm flipped his phone to speaker. "Yeah. In the car. Snake is with me. Que pasa?"

"Some fucker is attacking the farm," she said.

"What the fu..." His voice roared in his ears.

"Say again," Snake ordered, his voice colder than the air outside.

"Tom called. Heavy static, but I got the gist. People with guns. Jenna's gone for help. Sorry, man. Sam's been hit."

Snake growled, swerved out of his lane, scaring the guy behind shitless. "Is she..."

"Alive. Local law notified. Paramedics on the way."

His phone went dead. The hail and sleet beat on the roof. *Fucking shit reception.* It took all his control not to throw the damn thing out the window.

Storm scrubbed his fingers through his hair. "Shit, boss. I killed that son-of-a-bitch. How come he still gets to pull our goddam strings?" His voice tremored.

"No fucking idea." Their gazes locked briefly. "But think about it. We know he wasn't our Vermont shooter, the hit-and-run-driver, or the nut job who attacked Doc at the clinic."

Right. "I am going to kill the mother fucker." Storm's fists itched to punch a hole in something.

"Not if I reach him first." Snake countered.

The boss' eyes were filled with rage and fear that matched his own. Shoving every horrific image from his mind, Storm let go of the tension in his fingers as Snake swerved onto the verge. *What the...* A breath shuddered through him. "What you doing, man? Keep moving."

"Sam's pregnant," His friend's jaw clenched.

A tear grazed the side of a face, usually made of granite. *Shit.* "Get out. I'll drive." His phone rang again. "Hawke? You found Jenna?"

"No. It's Tom."

His gut wrenched at the hitch in the kid's voice. Storm shook his head and signaled for Snake to stay in his seat. "Hey, bud. You, okay? Mom back with you?"

"No."

If only he could reach through the phone and grab the kid. "How's Sam?"

"Okay. I think. She's talking to me."

Beside him, Snake let out an audible breath. "George?"

"Good. He's keeping guard at the door." After everything the kid had been through, he showed more strength than many Storm had met in service. "Stay inside and take care of Sam. Can you do that? We're on our way."

"Yes. Storm? I'm scared." His voice quivered.

"Me too, bud, but trust me, we've got this. Tell Sam her man is right here, and we're coming to get you." The phone went dead. He nodded at Snake. "You good to drive?"

"You bet. Frontal assault. Hard and fast. Shoot to kill. Fuck the questions." The boss growled.

The glimmer in his black eyes said it all. Anyone who dared lay a finger on their family had no chance of surviving the night. Storm nodded. "Fuck, yeah." Rage ran amok through his body. No place for the emotions warring in his head. *A baby.* His muscles tensed with a sense of dread. Breathing slow and deep, he willed himself to calm the hell down.

"Why didn't you say anything? About Sam. You guys being pregnant." Even now, he was having trouble imagining his friends as parents. They'd be amazing, but...

"It's early. Sam wanted to wait. Getting past the first three months is some sort of lucky charm," he choked.

"Congrats, man. Let's go get our women." This whole situation was surreal. He squeezed his friend's shoulder.

"Whoever made it past Sam has skills," Snake muttered, a vein bulging at his temple.

"Copy that." The boss' ex-military wife had bigger balls than all the Sentinel team put together. Storm's fist thumped the dash.

"Must be one of Hassan's assassins. Didn't receive the fucker's death notice."

The memory of Jen sitting on the beach at Coney Island, eating her dog with the lot, while he blurted the L word, kept him sane as they drove the last ten miles.

I'm coming, Doc. Stay alive.

***

J enna hid behind the tree, trying to catch her breath and settle her churning stomach. Any minute, she expected the man to come sloshing through the mud behind her.

George snarled, followed by rapid barking. Had the attackers made it into the house? Sam? Rain mingled with tears dripped off the end of her nose. Damn. Should she go back? *Pull it together.* Sam wouldn't hover behind a tree, scared to poke her nose out into the open.

All they had to do was stay alive until help came, except that wasn't bloody likely unless she found a landline and got help. Tom, her amazing brave boy, knew what to do if the tourniquet came loose, but Sam needed a hospital.

Above her head, branches creaked and groaned under the weight of the pounding rain and sleet. She rolled her lips a couple of times and darted into the open. Her feet pounded the undergrowth. Twigs and branches swept across her path, tricking her feet. The rain, heavier now, made it difficult to see very far ahead.

Running is pointless. The voice in her head screamed only a matter of time before they found her. But she'd never been a quitter. A deadly cocktail of terror laced with anger slipped through her bones and set her blood on fire. *Yes.* Jen, the woman Storm had shown her, had this covered.

Head down, she powered into the rain, driving her two steps back for each one she thrust forward. Her thighs cramped as she crested the small embankment and stumbled into the clearing. The exposed paddock stretched between her and the ribbon of smoke coming from the neighbor's chimney.

Jenna swiped a hand across her eyes. Temporarily blind, her damn foot found a ditch. Pain clawed at her ankle and in two seconds flat, she'd gone from a run to a limp.

Two silhouettes emerged from the mist. Jen hurled her body back the way she'd come. Stuck behind another tree, she held her breath. Had they seen her? *Please, God, no.* Pain radiated from her twisted ankle to her knee. She was pretty sure she hadn't broken it.

Crouching behind a fallen tree trunk, hands shaking, she pulled out her phone and checked for a signal. Still nothing. She prayed Tom had better luck.

The men moved closer. She could hear their footsteps splashing through the puddles. Resignation hung over her shoulders and a lump the size of Mount Rushmore stuck in her throat. If they found her, they'd kill her.

Snap out of it. She hadn't let Baxter win. Why give these guys the honor? Sam and Tom depended on her. She wouldn't let them down.

She patted her clothing, searched her pockets, looking for something pointy, anything to defend herself. Then she scanned her hands and fingers, stiff from the cold. Useless. Unlike Storm, she had no clue how to use them for self-defense. Rocks. Fallen branches. Slowly, she reached for the heaviest one she could handle, sucked in a huge breath and willed herself not to close her eyes.

Chapter Thirty-Nine

S torm jumped out, swung the gate open, and hopped back into his seat. "Go, go, go."

"We're too close, man." Snake turned off the engine. "We'll continue on foot."

The boss' feet hit the dirt. "Copy that." Storm growled. His insides quivered. Neither of them had a clue how many perps were out there. The team was on their way. Too far out to be of immediate help.

Local cops alerted. Great, but aside from the gun at their hip, their capabilities came nowhere close to their training or skills. Weapons drawn, head on a swivel, they hastened along the driveway.

Three hundred meters from the main house, Snake raised his fist, signaling for them to stop. The air buzzed. George howled. "You take care of Sam and Tom. I'm going after Jenna."

Snake nodded to his right. "Behind the kennels. It's the shortest way to Jed's."

Storm stayed close to the outbuildings and headed in the neighbor's direction. Several feet beyond the trees, the smell of tobacco mixed with the scent of wet pine needles. A few feet ahead, a ring of smoke drifted from behind a tree.

Storm flexed his fingers and edged closer and lined up behind the guy with a cigarette hanging from his mouth, taking a piss. He secured the idiot in a headlock, snapped his goddam neck and lowered the dumb mother fucker to the ground.

Wind howled through the trees. Behind him, moonlight strobed over the kennel rooftops before a gunshot, and Snake's "fuck you," blasted the night. So much for stealth.

Storm held his breath and waited for his surroundings to share their secrets. Damp twigs did their damndest to crack under heavy boots. Visible in his side vision, two men prowled toward a smaller figure. Jen, the woman who claimed his every fucking breath, dipped from the slim cover of the tree in front of him and yanked a branch, almost as big as her, off the ground.

Her head spun in his direction. "Storm?"

It took everything in him not to grab her and run, but the others were too close for them to make it very far. He placed his finger on his lips. *Shh, sweetheart. Not long now.*

Alert to her position, sensing the kill, the two men bounded straight for her and his whole body stilled. Cold rage ignited every cell in his body as he waited for the first guy to get within striking distance.

Storm hammered this throat with his elbow and sent him face down into the mud. On one knee beside the gurgling man, he plowed his fist three times into the fucker's face. Two more blows to the head shut him the hell up, for good. The coppery smell of fresh blood mingled with the lingering scent of bad breath.

Storm swung around to see the other man grab Jenna and twist her back to his front and use her as a shield. Jen screamed. The look on her pale face made him hungry to end this fucker with as much fucking pain as possible.

"Stay back, or I'll shoot," the man's voice trembled.

His heart stopped at the glint in Jen's eye right before she dropped the branch, and her elbow smacked her captor's nose. He cursed and threw her to the ground. If he wasn't so goddam terrified, he'd have laughed at the way his pint-sized Amazon took care of business.

"I'm going to cut off your balls and feed them to the dogs," Storm yelled. Head down, he charged. Launched onto the man's back and hammered the base of his skull with his fist.

But the shithead wasn't without skills. A judo flip and Storm flew over his shoulder. He jack-knifed to his feet and head butted the jerk's forehead. Stunned and disoriented, the guy swayed and spun on one foot. Storm caught him under the armpits and spread him on the ground. *Night sunshine.* As much as he wanted to crush his skull with his boot, they needed him alive.

"Oh, God." Jen croaked.

Clutching her stomach, she collapsed against the tree. "Jen, are you hurt?" His hands trembled as he took her by the shoulders and traced his fingers over her body, checking for any sign of blood.

"My ankle," she murmured.

"Let me see. He sank to his knees.

"It's okay, nothing broken." She burst into tears. "Oh, damn. I'm okay, honestly. Tom, Sam, they're at the house. We have to…"

He stood and brushed her forehead with his lips. "They're fine. Snake is with them."

Her breaths chugged in her chest. Afraid she may be more injured than he thought, he bent to gather her in his arms. "We need to get you to the hospital."

Above their heads, several shots struck the tree. *I knew I should have finished him.*

"Matt!"

"Down," he ordered and pushed Jenna to the ground.

Storm reared. Shielding Jenna with his body, he drew his knife. This time when shithead came at him, he ducked, rolled onto his back and caught the guy mid-lunge. He angled his blade to the left side of the man's chest and skewered the pig.

Pine needles crunched behind him. Blood roaring in his ears, he turned to take out the threat, only to see Jenna, palms out, trembling harder than the sleet hanging onto the branches. Her beautiful hazel eyes glassy with shock.

Shit. Did she think he'd harm her? "Jen, Jen." He gave her a gentle shake. "Look at me, sweetheart. I will never hurt you. It's over." Afraid she hadn't heard him, he stroked her arms, took hold of her hands, and thanked God he hadn't lost her forever. "I'm sorry you had to see that."

Storm sucked in a breath. Christ, he'd beg her forgiveness for letting any of this happen, but Snake, Sam leaning against his side, appeared. Tom walked a few steps behind them.

"Mum." Tom charged ahead and threw his arms around Jenna.

"Oh, God. You're safe. I love you." Jen drew her son to her and showered him with kisses. Fresh tears glistened in her eyes.

"Mum," he groaned, his cheeks turning crimson.

With a chuckle, Storm hugged and kissed them both, lingering a little longer on Jen's soft lips.

"Aww." Tom jabbed him in the ribs. "We love you, too."

"For heaven's sake, I love you, and you, and you, but mostly you." Sam cradled her injured arm and smiled at Snake. "Crazy close to a hippie love fest."

Tom lifted his head and stared at the two bodies. "Hey, that's the guy who gave us directions at the snow."

"Figures." Snake muttered.

"Man. I'm ready for a hot shower. First, you two need a hospital," he squeezed Jen to him. "Then home."

***

Two months later.

"Right here." Matt pointed to her foot, then to his knee.

"Mmm. Nurse Storm suits you," Jen smiled as he lifted her leg and kissed her cheek with tenderness, he usually did his best to hide. Not that it worked with her and Tom, or any of his Sentinel family.

The tip of his calloused finger swiped a stray hair from the corner of her mouth. The slight roughness felt good as he cupped her head and his arms tightened around her.

Curled in his arms, she nuzzled his shoulder and immediately missed the silver-gray eyes that always left her breathless. Jenna tilted her head and stared into the heavy-lidded gaze of her future.

Storm leaned in for a deeper kiss that set off a tingling low in her belly. "Again." Her fingers clutched his T-shirt.

"And again, and again. I'll never get tired of kissing you." His hand slid from the back of her neck and palmed her jaw. The edge of his thumb skirting the edge of her mouth until she opened for him. His tongue slipped inside and slowly circled her mouth. A tease. A promise.

The buzzing between her ears grew louder, the desire to have him right there on the couch washing through her blood and making her head pound.

"Let's take this upstairs." His eyes turned the color of clouds right before the heavens opened.

"Oops, my bad. Sorry to interrupt, but Jake's here. I'm off." Tom said, his head poking around the open door.

Storm shuffled away. Breathless, Jenna gaped at the self-assured, bold man, who protected her with his bare hands more than once, embarrassed by a mouthy teenager, as if someone had caught him snogging his prom date under the bleachers.

"Sure darling. Take care, stay safe." This was the first time she'd let him out of her sight for weeks. Jen swallowed the tears threatening to spill.

"Yeah, call me if you guys need a ride." Storm cleared his throat.

The door clicked shut. *Yes.* Thank Christ for weekend stopovers. Tom was gone until tomorrow afternoon. She wiggled her foot until her big toe nudged at the bulge behind Storm's zipper.

Strong fingers kneaded her ankle, careful to avoid the bandage. Not quite the reaction she'd been looking for, but the house was theirs. No need to duck for the bedroom. Massage as foreplay before they sank to the floor?

"Forgive me?" His gaze flicked from her face to her big toe.

Did her feet smell? "Always?" She stilled his fingers and kissed his palm. "Are we talking specifics?"

"I don't deserve you, or Tom. Family." The corners of his eyes glistened.

Jenna broke out in a cold sweat. "Where are you right now? A moment ago, you were kissing me senseless. And now you're enthralled by my big toe. And not in a good way. I thought we were past all this.

"I failed to protect you. Too many times." Storm rasped. His Adam's apple jumped.

"Nope." Jenna grabbed his wrist, her body trembling, afraid she wouldn't be able to stop him from leaping off the couch. His turn to run. No way.

"Nope?" Storm echoed.

"You heard me. Nope. As in, never go there again. You protected me, us, in the snow, the clinic." She tilted her head. "At the farm. You came for us. I never doubted it for a second. Neither did Tom. He said you were the first person he called?" Jen straightened her spine. "I am mad at you, though."

Storm nodded. Jen groaned, and when his sad, sorry eyes found hers, her heart slammed against her chest. Hoisting her backside off the couch, she straddled his thighs. "Christine, dummy. What are we going to do about her?"

The proverbial elephant in the room sat its gigantic arse next to them and the Earth swayed.

"She's my problem, sweetheart. Never yours."

"See, that right there is why you drive me bonkers." The way his mouth quivered, as if he couldn't decide whether to laugh, gave her hope. "If me and Tom are sticking around, understand this. No more dividing up responsibilities as though they were a bloody birthday cake. *We* will help her. Understood?" Jenna cupped his cheeks. "I love you."

"Jen," he whispered. "My oath, sweetheart. I love you. Only you."

"Great. Now we've got that cleared up. Dry your eyes, Nurse Storm, and get back to loving my foot."

Epilogue

Four Months later

"I can't believe Sam's having a baby." Jenna sighed and leaned her head against Storm's shoulder.

"Seriously, sweetheart, we need to talk." Storm raised an eyebrow at the most gorgeous woman in the room.

"Shut up. You know what I mean." Jen punched his arm, sending a bolt of electricity zapping through him.

With the threat from Hassan obliterated, everyone was at the farm for Sam's baby shower. The women were off smudging the entire farm, clearing the air before the kid arrived, while the guys kicked back round the fire, killing a few long necks.

New beginnings. And as much as he loved hanging with this crowd, he'd rather be attending a different type of shower, getting wet and naked with Doc. But Jen, clothed, nestled to his side, came in at a great second.

"Where's Trig? I thought he'd be here by now." Sam asked, leading her posse to the fire.

"Dunno," Storm replied. "He was supposed to tag along with us but sent a message saying to push on without him. Didn't give a reason."

"Forgot his present," Tom offered.

Sam laughed. "Not another teddy bear."

Snake pulled her onto his lap, arms locked around her. "Miss me." He nuzzled the side of her neck.

"Time to go?" Jen batted her eyelashes.

"You read my mind. Let's grab the kid," he drawled, linking their fingers. "Let's get wet. One arm slung around Jen's shoulder, he caught Tom's eye and nodded at the door.

"Hey where are you taking your woman?" Snake called after them.

His woman. Hell, yeah. Best two words in the English language Almost. "Marry me."

"Are you joking?"

If the sun hadn't caught the twinkle in Jen's eye, her laugh might have scared him. "Never been more serious in my life." He hooked Tom around the neck. "Want me to ask Tom's permission first?"

"No. I mean, maybe. How many babies do you want?" Again, with the twinkle.

This time, every other person in the room, including Tom, shared her laugh. "How about we start with four?"

"Perfect. Make it a yes. Of course, I'll marry you."

Storm scooped Jen into his arms. He reckoned she'd keep him busy making her the happiest woman on the planet, making kissing memories. "Later, friends."

Eliza Renton

Thank you for reading Storm and Jenna's story. It took me longer to than I anticipated, but I hope I've done them justice. Next in the Series is Trigger's story. I've started, and he's a bit darker than some of the others despite his cocky humor.

LOVE TAKES COURAGE

Eliza Renton writes Romantic Suspense featuring alpha protectors and the women who win their hearts. She is a card-carrying pluviophile who enjoys walking, gardening, and eating ice cream in the rain. When she is not deep in the editing cave or listening to her characters, she hangs out with her knitting group or binge-watches action-packed films and TV.

Eliza thinks the best part of being a writer is visiting make-believe worlds and falling in love while others stress about parking, their boss, or the cost of a cup of coffee.

If you would like to sign up for my newsletter or check out some of my other books you can find me on Facebook, Instagram and occasionally TikTok or why not take a look at my website. https://www.elizarenton.com.

Happy reading. Eliza.